The Heartbreaker

AMISH COUNTRY BRIDES

Jennifer Spredemann

www.jenniferspredemann.com

Published in Indiana by *Blessed Publishing*.

www.jenniferspredemann.com

All Scripture quotations are taken from the *King James Version* of the *Holy Bible*.

Cover design by *iCreate Designs* ©

ISBN: 978-1-940492-51-3
10 9 8 7 6 5 4 3 2 1

Get a FREE short story as my thank you gift to you when you sign up for my newsletter here:
www.jenniferspredemann.com

BOOKS by JENNIFER SPREDEMANN

Learning to Love – Saul's Story
(Sequel to Chloe's Revelation)

AMISH BY ACCIDENT TRILOGY
Amish by Accident
Englisch on Purpose (Prequel to *Amish by Accident*)
Christmas in Paradise (Sequel to *Amish by Accident*) (co-authored with Brandi Gabriel)

AMISH SECRETS SERIES
An Unforgivable Secret - Amish Secrets 1
A Secret Encounter - Amish Secrets 2
A Secret of the Heart - Amish Secrets 3
An Undeniable Secret - Amish Secrets 4
A Secret Sacrifice - Amish Secrets 5 (co-authored with Brandi Gabriel)
A Secret of the Soul - Amish Secrets 6
A Secret Christmas – Amish Secrets 2.5 (co-authored with Brandi Gabriel)

AMISH BIBLE ROMANCES
An Amish Reward (Isaac)
An Amish Deception (Jacob)
An Amish Honor (Joseph)
An Amish Blessing (Ruth)
An Amish Betrayal (David)

Unofficial Glossary
of Pennsylvania Dutch Words

Ach – Oh

Alt maedel – Old maid

Bann – Shunning

Boppli/Bopplin – Baby/Babies

Bruder/Brieder – Brother/Brothers

Bu – Boy

Daed/Dat – Dad

Dawdi – Grandfather

Denki – Thanks

Der Herr – The Lord

Dochder – Daughter

Dummkopp – Dummy

Englischer – A non-Amish person

Ferhoodled – Mixed up

Fraa – Wife

G'may – Members of an Amish fellowship

Gott – God

Gross sohn – Grandson

Gut – Good

Jah – Yes

Kapp – Amish head covering

Kinner – Children

Kumm – Come
Maed/Maedel – Girls/Girl
Mamm – Mom
Mammi – Grandmother
Mei fraa – My wife
Ordnung – Rules of the Amish community
Rumspringa – Running around period for Amish youth
Schatzi – Sweetheart
Schweschder(n) – Sister(s)
Sehr gut – Very good
Wunderbaar – Wonderful

Author's Note

The Amish/Mennonite people and their communities differ one from another. There are, in fact, no two Amish communities exactly alike. It is this premise on which this book is written. I have taken cautious steps to assure the authenticity of Amish practices and customs. Old Order Amish and New Order Amish may be portrayed in this work of fiction and may differ from some communities. Although the book may be set in a certain locality, the practices featured in the book may not necessarily reflect that particular district's beliefs or culture. This book is purely fictional and built around a fictional community, even though you may see similarities to real-life people, practices, and occurrences.

We, as *Englischers*, can learn a lot from the Plain People and their simple way of life. Their hard work, close-knit family life, and concern for others are to be applauded. As the Lord wills, may this special culture continue to be respected and remain so for many centuries to come, and may the light of God's salvation reach their hearts.

ONE

The sun's fingers stretched through the panes of Miriam Yoder's bedroom window, caressing her face in warm bliss. *Ach*, today would be a beautiful day. A welcome break from the recent storms they'd been having. She knelt next to her bed, as she did each morning, and bowed her head. She had a lot to be thankful for. A *gut* family, friends, the *wunderbaar* sunshine, and not having to see *his* face.

She shouldn't think that, and she certainly shouldn't pray it. But she couldn't help it. She *was* thankful that she didn't have to see Michael Eicher's face at every gathering their church district had. She was happy she no longer had to gaze into his mesmerizing eyes or glimpse his irresistible smile. She was glad that he'd jumped the fence, providing surety that he wouldn't terrorize her heart anymore. Never again. Not him, or any other man, for that matter.

At least, if she stayed single, she didn't have to worry about fixing three square meals a day and waiting on a husband hand and foot. She didn't have to worry about caring for sick children like her friends occasionally did. It was a blessing, actually, that Michael Eicher had forced hard-earned wisdom upon her.

If only she could believe that. She knew that she should have forgiven him by now. She knew that she should just forget everything that happened. But doing so seemed impossible. Especially in light of—

"Miriam!" *Mamm's* voice called from downstairs, breaking through her meandering thoughts.

"Coming, *Mamm*." She frowned, then whispered a hastened, "Amen." She'd have to send the remainder of her prayer heavenward while *Daed* prayed at breakfast time. Surely, *Der Herr* would understand.

She threw her choring dress on in record time, then haphazardly pinned up her hair with her work kerchief as her covering. No need to don her best for the chickens.

Hopefully *Mamm* hadn't started preparing the morning meal without her. She had to pull her weight if she intended to stay in her folks' home. She supposed that she could move out, since she was plenty old enough, but that would likely be too lonely. Besides, she didn't need idle time. Time to think about *him*. *Ach*, if only she could erase him from her memory altogether. He certainly hadn't given a second thought to her. If only he'd never taken her on that first buggy ride. Or the second. Or the third. If only...*stop!*

"Will you gather the eggs from the hen house?" *Mamm* asked the second Miriam's feet hit the bottom step.

"*Jah*. It seems they've been laying other places lately too. I found some in the woodshed the other day, and some up in the loft when *Daed* had me fetch hay."

"In the loft even?" *Mamm* stared at her as though she held answers. "It wonders me how they would get up yonder."

Miriam shrugged. "I guess they must've flown up there. They are birds, ain't so?" She opened the back door, egg basket in hand, but paused to hear *Mamm's* words before stepping out.

"Unless one of your *brieder* put one of the poor creatures up there."

Jah, there was that. Her nine-year-old brother Benny did possess an ornery streak. Hopefully, he'd have the sense not to turn out like...

Why in the world could she not dispel Michael

Eicher from her thoughts today? It wasn't like she'd pined after him all these years he'd been gone. *Nee*, quite the opposite. As far as she was concerned, good-for-nothing Michael Eicher could jump off a bridge. Or get thrown from a buggy. Or... *ach*, I'm sorry, *Gott*. That was *not* a charitable thought, whether Michael Eicher was worthy of one or not.

She pressed her lips together, determined to distract herself.

"Hey, chickens. Do you have any eggs for me to find today?" She smiled at the creatures as she headed toward the hen house.

∞

Michael Eicher's eyes fluttered open. *Ach*, he'd slept great. He turned over on his side, not the least bit surprised to find the spot next to him empty. The beautiful woman he'd met last night—what was her name? Casey? Cathy? Cassy?—must have gone already. He yawned and stretched. What time was it anyway?

He sat up and reached for his cell phone. *Almost nine? Oh shoot, I'm late for work. Again.* No doubt that was where what's-her-name had gone. And *she* probably hadn't been late.

He hurried and threw on his jeans, then tugged his

arms into his work shirt. While sprinting to the kitchen to find a quick bite to swallow on his way to work, he buttoned up his shirt. He spotted a note on his tiny kitchen table.

Thanks for the fun! Call me some time. – Cassidy

So *that* was her name! Not that it mattered. He'd likely never see her again. He had a maximum two-date rule. If he didn't get what he wanted by then, he moved on. Fortunately, Cassidy had no problem providing for his wants on the first date.

In his younger days, when he still lived in his Plain community, he'd once taken the same woman on a buggy ride five times in a row. *Five* times? He rubbed his stubbled cheek and shook his head, still amazed. What had he been thinking? He hadn't. He'd nearly lost himself, his dating standards—if that's what one could call it—to her. He closed his eyes, attempting to recall her name. He knew it well but his brain was in a fog this morning, likely from indulging in too much drink the night before.

Miriam. Miri. Jah, she was the one. As soon as he realized he'd been losing himself—his heart—he moved on. A ride or two with someone else after her, then out of the community for good. No need to make attachments to a community he wouldn't be staying in. But *Miri, mmm*, she had been in a league of her own.

He glanced at Cassidy's note again. The words were written in a large heart, along with her phone number. He crumpled the paper and tossed it in the trash. *No, thank you.*

He grabbed a slice of bread and slathered peanut butter on it, which made him long for the peanut butter spread he'd grown up with in his Amish community. Perhaps he'd get the recipe for it if he ever returned home again. It had been a couple of years since he'd visited his *grossdawdi*—his only tie to the community now. He took a bite of his snack and grunted. It would have to suffice till his lunch break.

He patted his pocket to be sure his wallet and motorcycle key were still safely tucked away in his jeans, then ran out the door. He really should have showered this morning, but there was no time. He was already late.

Hopefully, Nick would be forgiving of his tardiness. He knew he'd been getting on his boss's nerves lately. This would be the second time he was late this week. Perhaps he and whatever-her-name-was should have left the night club a little earlier. Oh well, too late now.

He revved the bike and weaved in and out of traffic, then finally came to a screeching halt at the mechanic shop he'd worked at for the last two months.

"Don't bother clocking in, Mike. You're fired." Nick shook his head in disappointment as Michael walked toward him.

"But I—"

"Don't even attempt any excuses. I saw your bike out at Jean's last night. And I saw you leaving with a woman."

"I need this job, Nick."

"Not my problem." He shook his head. "You stink. Did you not even bother to shower this morning?"

"I was running late." He lifted his arm and took a whiff. Nick was right. He had trouble outgrowing some of the old habits he'd learned growing up in his strict Amish community. He'd only been allowed a bath once a week on Saturdays, and before a special occasion, such as a wedding. It wasn't so bad when you lived in an Amish community and everyone else carried the same hard work stench. But shortly after he'd left, he learned the *Englisch* went by different standards where cleanliness was concerned, among other things.

"Your breath too, man." Nick frowned. "How on earth did you lure a woman home?"

Michael smiled fully, crossed his muscled arms over his chest, and raised his eyebrows.

"I guess girls will give pretty boys just about anything." Nick shrugged.

That, he'd been right about. He'd seldom been turned down, and he attributed that to his good looks, hard-earned body, and extroverted personality. If his good looks couldn't win a woman over, his congeniality would. He'd become a genius at flattery. *Jah*, from a woman's perspective, he was a fine catch. He'd been told as much nearly every time he was with a woman. He chuckled to himself. They thought he was the perfect catch, but they quickly found out he was only into catch and release. No ball and chain. No strings attached.

"My breath was fine last night." He grinned. "I had a mint."

"More like a mint julep." Nick rolled his eyes. "You know, if I were you, I'd rethink my life."

And back to the issue at hand. His fingers practically screeched through his oily hair. "Seriously, man. You're not *really* firing me, are you?"

"Yeah. I'm *really* firing you." Nick nodded. "Don't bother putting me as a reference on your next job application. I will tell them the truth."

"Which is?" He swallowed, not sure he wanted to hear his boss's—make that *ex*-boss's—evaluation.

"You're a decent worker—when you actually show up. I need to get back to work."

His gaze followed Nick's to a vehicle that had just

pulled in to the shop. "But I need this job!"

"Sorry. But I warned you, Mike."

"Give me another chance. Please!"

"You're out of chances. I gave you two. It was two too many. I run a mechanic shop, not a daycare. I don't have time for workers who don't pull their weight. It makes me look incompetent to my customers, and that's the last thing a business owner wants. I value other people's time. You should too. It's called respect." Nick turned and walked back to the bay.

Michael let out a string of obscenities.

"Like I said." Nick hollered. "Rethink your life. Don't come back. Your check will be in the mail."

He stomped to his bike and peeled out of the parking lot. He could slam his fist up against a wall right about now. How could life be great and stink at the same time? How on earth was he going to pay rent now?

TWO

Michael stared down at the newspaper, combing the Help Wanted ads for anything he might be qualified for. Only two jobs appealed to him and he'd already applied for both. The employers had been eager to meet him at first—his good looks had provided many opportunities over the years—until they studied his job history. Then it was always the same. *Why did you only work at such-and-such for a few months? Why did you leave?* He'd considered lying on the last answer and saying he wasn't fired, but the one time he did, they'd called his former employer and received the truth. After that, he'd basically been thrown out on his ear.

Ach, it seemed he'd been fired as many times as he'd been hired. *Dawdi* would not be pleased. Amish were known for their work ethic. Apparently,

Michael didn't inherit that gene. He didn't relish disappointing his grandfather, but he couldn't help having ants in his pants. And if he couldn't find work, he'd have to go back home and ask *Dawdi* for money to pay his rent—something he loathed to even think about.

Dawdi would give him money, but only after he worked for him. His grandfather was a man of principle and didn't believe in handouts. *Nee*, his *grossdawdi* lived by the motto *if a man doesn't work, a man doesn't eat*. At least he'd be allowed to *kumm* back and live in *Dawdi's* home until he got back on his feet. He'd done it a couple other times within the past five years, so *Dawdi* would likely be expecting him soon. Unlike the others in the community, *Dawdi* didn't shun him—at least not in his own home. Michael had been thankful for that.

He didn't know what he'd do without his *grossdawdi*. That was a circumstance he did not want to ever dwell on. Out of all the people in his family, *Dawdi* had always been the one to accept him no matter what.

Michael suspected *Dawdi* held out hope that one day he'd return to the Amish fold for good. But Michael knew that would never happen. The Amish life had too many restrictions on just about everything. He wasn't going to let a few power-hungry men dictate how he lived his life. It just wasn't going to happen.

Michael revved his bike, daring to veer around the corners at heart-racing speeds. He loved the adrenaline that accompanied hard living, and the rush of wind through his hair. It reminded him of a certain woman who used to run her fingers through it when it had been longer. Why so many thoughts of Miriam Yoder lately? Probably because he'd been pondering visiting his *grossdawdi*. He hadn't seen her in forever, it seemed.

He dreamt of her now, wondering if she was married. If she was, then her last name would no longer be Yoder, he mused. *Jah*, she likely was. Not that he'd let something like that deter him if he ever wanted to see her again. He'd learned that the married women at the clubs were usually just as willing as the others. It shouldn't be much more difficult with Miri. Sure, she was Amish, but that didn't matter. He'd just have to step carefully. Hopefully, her husband worked away from the home. That would make it easy.

Out of all the Plain women he'd dated, she had been

his favorite conquest. A beautiful woman indeed. A face as attractive as his own, soft intoxicating long hair, curves in all the right places... *Jah*, if he ever returned to his former Amish community, he'd definitely be seeking her out.

When he felt the tire slipping, his attention snapped back to the road. He glanced down and noticed the grass clippings just as his motorcycle slid out from under him. His eyes squeezed shut, as he attempted to protect himself from the intense pain he was likely to endure.

"I'm leaving now," Miriam called to *Mamm* from the door.

"Have a *gut* day, *dochder*. Tell Sammy hello for us."

"*Jah*, I will." She stepped outside into the crisp morning air. The short walk to the older man's house was always one of her favorite parts of the day. It was her time alone to commune with God. She would thank Him for His blessings and ask His guidance throughout the day.

She thought of the list Sammy had given her for the week. Grocery shopping. Purchasing vegetable plants from the Troyers' greenhouse for his garden, then planting them. Fixing supper. All stuff she loved to do, especially for Sammy. He'd been somewhat of a *grossdawdi* to her after her own grandfather had passed away a few years ago. She relished the times they would sit out on the porch and talk. Although she'd loved her own *grossdawdi*, Sammy owned a special place in her heart. He'd been one of the kindest souls she'd ever known. She felt like she could share anything with him, although she hadn't shared her deepest secrets. *Nee*, some things were just too personal—only things she could disclose to *Der Herr*.

Miriam opened the screen door and knocked. There was no answer.

Strange. Sammy usually had his door opened this time of day, with just the screen closed to let the breeze in. "Sammy?"

She knocked once more.

Where was he? He'd usually come to the door by this time. Perhaps he was occupied. She'd give him a few minutes before she knocked again, just in case he was taking care of personal business. She dropped down onto the porch swing and pushed the wooden floor board with her toes, setting the swing in gentle motion.

Five minutes later, she knocked again, with no response.

Then she decided to check the barn and the pasture

to see if his driving horse was in his stall or out grazing. She discovered the barn was empty, but sure enough Dr. Seuss was out in the field. She'd laughed when Sammy had first told her his horse's name. He said that one of his grandchildren named the horse after their favorite children's author. Oh well, she supposed it was better than naming the poor creature *Green Eggs and Ham* or *The Cat in the Hat*, which was what the child wanted to name him. So, Dr. Seuss it was.

A ring pealed through the air and she turned her attention to the phone shanty between Sammy's and his neighbor's property. She jogged toward it, but the ringing had long ceased by the time she arrived. The answering machine's light was flashing, so she pushed Play.

Sammy's voice echoed through the line, "Hello, this message is for Miriam Yoder. This is Sammy. I'm at the hospital right now. Don't worry, it's not for me. I am fine. *Chust* visiting someone. I should be back home in a couple of days. If you need to get inside the house, you know where I usually leave the key. I guess I won't be needing you to make me any meals right now. At least not for a couple of days. I left a list on the table for you. See you when I get back."

She erased the message and then frowned, thinking of Sammy's words. Who could be in the hospital? She hadn't heard that anyone in the community had sustained an injury or of anyone requiring hospitalization.

A frown tugged her lips downward. The thought of Sammy being away dampened her spirits a bit. He'd always had a smile and word of encouragement for her. She'd miss him. Nevertheless, she breathed a quick prayer for whomever he was visiting in the hospital, and that Sammy would return safely and soon.

After finishing her tasks at Sammy's, she'd make a quick stop in at her best friend Nora's place. She and Nora had pretty much been great friends since they'd met, except for the small rift they'd had when Miriam dated Michael. Miriam had been unaware that her friend had ridden home with him prior to asking her. Like every other girl, Nora had a crush on him. When rumors began flying around about Michael and Miriam being a couple, Nora completely wrote her off as a friend.

When Michael ended his courtship with Miriam, she'd been left without her beau and her best friend. Heartbroken over the entire ordeal, Miriam fled to the *Englisch* world, nursing her bleeding heart. After Miriam returned to their community a year and a half later, she discovered that Nora had moved on and married.

A couple weeks after Miriam's return, her friend showed up asking forgiveness, so they'd made amends. Miriam was glad to resume their friendship, but she'd never fully recovered from either wound. The scars remained.

THREE

A beep, beep, beep sound forced Michael's eyes to drift open, but his vision was hazy. He'd slept well but it was time to get up now. Time to go job hunting yet again. He blindly felt for his alarm clock to shut it off. Where was it?

He lifted himself off the pillow only to discover intense pain pounding his head. Now that he'd awakened more, he was conscious of pain in his entire body. He forced his eyes to open all the way and noticed his arm in a cast and his leg suspended in a sling in the air. *Ach*, the hospital.

Motorcycle accident. *Jah*, that was it.

He attempted to sit up again.

"*Nee*, you stay right there."

The familiar voice grabbed his attention. "*Dawdi*?" He turned his head toward the voice. Sure enough, his grandfather sat on a chair next to his bed.

"What are you doing here?"

"I think you mean what are *you* doing here? They called me from your phone. Said something about ice."

"Ice? Oh, yeah, in case of emergency. *Jah*, your number is down for that."

"You will come home with me to recover."

"What is wrong with me? How long have I been here?"

"A couple of days." His *grossdawdi* sighed. "Your leg and arm are broken. The doctor said they will need to be in a cast for six weeks. You have a slight concussion. Other than that, you *chust* have a few bumps and bruises. You have much to thank *Der Herr* for. It could have been much worse."

He refrained from sneering at *Dawdi's* mention of the alleged Man Upstairs. He had no use for God or His *thou shalt nots*. "When can I leave?"

"As soon as you learn to get around, they said."

He forgot about his injured arm and tried to lift it. He groaned as pain shot through to his shoulder. "Six weeks?" He grimaced trying to catch his breath. "What am I going to do for six weeks?"

"You will continue your recovery. And you will help out on the farm."

He thought about his *grossdawdi's* farm. A little bit

of fresh air might do him some good. "Do you still have than ornery rooster?"

Dawdi chuckled. "As feisty as ever."

He grunted. "I think I'll let you gather the eggs then."

"*Nee*, I have a helper now."

"A helper?"

"A *maedel* that comes over to help me out."

"Ooh...a young woman?" He grinned like a fool. "Do I know her?"

"Perhaps. But you're in no condition to be thinking about *maed* right now."

"*Ach*, that's practically *all* I think about."

His *grossdawdi* frowned. "That is not *gut*. *Der Herr* should be in the middle of your thoughts."

He nearly snorted, but refrained out of respect for *Dawdi*. How long had it been since he'd entertained coherent thoughts of a Higher Power? A long, long time, it seemed. He kept silent on the matter.

"What about my apartment? My stuff?" He frowned.

"Your landlord was going to put it in storage, but I suggested my barn instead. He's charging you a fifty-dollar moving fee."

"Figures." He thought of the items he owned. Some things he'd never want his *grossdawdi* to see or know about. Hopefully, his landlord threw everything into boxes and his private stuff was hidden. *Ach*, he'd be embarrassed if *Dawdi* ever looked through his things. He'd never ever approve. If he had his way, *Dawdi* would never see it. He wished he could call his landlord and ask him to throw it out.

Heat rose up his neck. "You, uh, you haven't gone through it. Have you?" He swallowed hard.

"*Nee*, it is not mine."

He released a sigh of relief. "I can pay you for storage."

"Nonsense. You can't even work a job in your condition. How do you plan to pay for storage?"

"I'll get another job eventually."

"You can work for your *grossdawdi* for room and board."

"And meals?"

"*Jah, mei maedel* occasionally makes meals. I'm sure she won't mind cooking for two." *Dawdi* raised a brow. "But for the most part, we'll be cooking for ourselves."

"And her name is?"

"You will meet her soon enough. For now, you rest and concentrate on getting better."

"Will you at least tell me how old she is? She's not a school girl or anything, is she?"

"*Ach*, you dream about *maed* way too much. *Nee*, I believe she's close to your age. And that's all I will say." He shook his head. "It does not matter, though. You are still living in the *Englisch* world. She will have no interest in you. She is a *gut* Amish girl."

Clearly, his *grossdawdi* underestimated his persuasion skills when it came to women. He'd had very few failures in that department. Usually, all it took was a gaze, a wink, and a friendly conversation to get his way. He was quite confident this encounter wouldn't be much different, Amish *maedel* or no.

His lips curved upward. The sooner he left this hospital, the better. Of course, he *had* seen a cute nurse walk by. Maybe he could get her number.

"You returning home with me is contingent on one thing." *Dawdi* scratched his scraggly beard as he walked beside Michael in the hospital's hall. It was only a brief exercise, with more distance added each day.

"What's that?"

"You must attend church."

Michael shrugged with his one good shoulder. "I already figured you'd insist on that."

"You're sure to attract plenty of attention with

your leg in a cast and your arm in that sling."

"Ah, I don't mind."

His *grossdawdi* chuckled. "That's what I figured. You always liked being the center of attention."

And that was the truth. Especially when it came to women. "True."

"It's not a *gut* thing. I'm afraid your good looks have been a curse to you."

"Oh, no, *Dawdi*. You've got it all wrong."

"How's that?"

"That's why it's so easy to get women." His grin widened and his eyebrows rose twice over.

"*Jah*, but it has caused you to sin. Made you full of pride. Taken you away from *Der Herr* and His people." *Dawdi* eyed him dubiously. "You should only have one woman."

He almost choked. "One? You're serious?"

"That is what *Der Herr* says."

They both turned the corner and stepped back into his hospital room. "Yeah, well, I believe in living by my own code of conduct."

"Is that what you call it?" He frowned.

"Yep."

Dawdi stared at him. "But you will answer to *Gott* someday."

"Maybe." He released his crutch, then hoisted

himself onto the bed with *Dawdi's* help.

"There's no maybe."

"I'm good, *Dawdi*. You don't need to worry about me."

Dawdi sighed, then turned quiet.

Michael pulled the sheet to his torso. "I'm exhausted. Do you mind if I try to catch some Z's?"

"No, go ahead. I have something I need to do anyhow."

Michael guessed the "something" his *grossdawdi* was referring to was praying for his wayward grandson. He watched as *Dawdi* walked out the door with his shoulders slumped. He hadn't meant to discourage his grandfather, but he didn't want to encourage false hope either. He'd stay with his *grossdawdi* until he was better, but he had absolutely no desire to return to the Amish church.

FOUR

Miriam had always enjoyed church Sundays. Well, *almost* always. After she'd returned from the *Englisch* world, she'd harbored a tremendous amount of guilt. Even after being baptized, her soul remained unsettled. Her burden had lightened just slightly. Lightened, but hadn't lifted completely. Because there were some things in her past that she'd been too ashamed to admit, especially to her fellow Amish community. She'd confessed her sins to *Der Herr*, but outwardly she lived a lie. She was not the righteous saint the *g'may* believed her to be. *Nee*, far from it.

Despite her self-deprecation, she still derived joy from attending the bi-monthly get-togethers. She'd learned to fix her focus on *Gott*, and tune out the condemning voices in her head. She knew *Der Herr* had forgiven her. Was it really anyone else's business,

27

given the fact that she'd already made things right with the One who truly mattered? She thought not.

But she knew what was expected. Total transparency. And that, she had not yielded to.

As soon as she descended her folks' carriage, she made a beeline for the Petersheims' kitchen. Loaf of bread in hand, she walked through the door. The women seemed awfully chatty this morning. Had something happened in the community?

Nora grasped her arm the moment she set the bread on the counter and guided her to a private place. Miriam couldn't decipher her friend's expression. "Did you know he was coming?"

Miriam frowned. "What? Who?"

Nora dragged her over to the window and pointed at the black-clad men standing in a semi-circle near the barn.

Miriam squinted into the bright morning light. "I don't—"

"It's Michael Eicher. The one with the crutch."

Miriam's heart pounded. "*What*?"

"So you *didn't* know?"

"I had no idea." She shook her head. "Why is he here? And what's wrong with him?"

"Seems that Sammy brought him home from the hospital. Motorcycle accident." Nora rolled her eyes.

Apparently, there hadn't been any love lost between them.

"Oh, wow. I knew Sammy was visiting someone in the hospital, but I never thought—"

"Stay away from him, Miriam. You know what he's like."

She heard the warning tone in her friend's voice loud and clear.

"Oh, believe me, I know. And I don't plan on getting anywhere near him if I can help it." She sighed. "But...is he staying at Sammy's? If so, I don't know how I'm going to avoid him. I work for Sammy."

"Maybe you should stop."

"Stop? But Sammy needs my help. Probably even more so if he has to spend his time caring for his *gross sohn*."

"I don't like it."

"Neither do I. But if he's the same Michael we know, he won't be staying a minute longer than he has to. I highly doubt he has any intentions of returning."

"Just watch your step. I know how persuasive he can be."

Jah. So did she. She knew it all too well. And as much as she could help it, she'd stay far away from handsome Michael Eicher. She couldn't afford to allow his charms to sweep her off her feet ever again.

As he stood with the men prior to meeting, Michael glanced around the Petersheims' property, mentally identifying several women he'd briefly dated. He smirked, wondering how many of these men surrounding him knew he'd likely claimed their wives before they had. Several of the women's gazes flitted in his direction, their cheeks immediately darkening when their eyes met. *Jah*, this would be fun.

He noticed Miriam worked amongst the married women, helping bring food items into the Petersheims' home. *Ach*, he knew it. He studied her, hoping to see which man her eyes honed in on. It would be much easier if he knew which man was her husband so he could find out all the essential information he needed, like where he worked and what his hours were. After watching her for several minutes, he still couldn't figure it out. Perhaps she and her husband didn't get along well. *Jah*, that could work to his advantage for sure.

"Mike? Michael Eicher, is that you?" One of the young men he'd hung out with in *rumspringa* smiled and clasped his uninjured shoulder.

"*Jah*." *Ach*, what was his name?

"Peter Stoltzfus. Remember?"

"Pete. *Jah*. *Jah*, of course." He and Pete had spent many hours together, mostly getting into trouble.

Pete had a full beard that indicated he was married. "You're married, ain't so?"

"*Jah*." He nodded across the yard and his eyes connected with a young woman sitting on the porch swing holding a baby in her arms. "Sandy Mae."

Michael frowned, trying to recollect the woman, but she didn't look familiar to him. Her name didn't ring a bell either.

"She and her family moved here from Iowa about five years ago," Pete explained.

Michael nodded. That would have been about the time he'd left for the *Englisch* world. He studied Pete's *fraa*. She was pretty good looking. Just not as gorgeous as Miriam.

Pete's elbow slammed into Michael's side. "Don't get any ideas. It won't go well for you."

Michael frowned at his former friend. "Hey, that wasn't necessary."

"I mean it, Mike. I know your reputation. I've heard the stories."

"*Jah*?" Michael's brow lifted and he smirked. "Stories, huh?"

"None good. There was even a rumor..." his voice trailed off.

"A rumor?"

His waved his hand in front of his face. "*Ach,*

forget I said anything. Just mind your behavior."

Michael chuckled. "Yeah, I'll do that."

"You planning on making a confession?" Apparently, his sarcasm was lost on Pete.

He sneered.

"I'll take that as a no." Pete shook his head. "Figures. Listen, I meant what I said. Stay away from my *fraa*."

"Not a problem. I have somebody else on my mind."

He suddenly wished he could be a fly on the wall. If Pete knew his reputation, surely many of these people were talking about him at this very moment. Was Miriam? His eyes focused on her and he waited until she looked at him. Except she hadn't. Not even once. He frowned. Maybe he'd seek her out after the common meal or catch her glancing his way during the service.

He leaned over and whispered to Pete. "Who is Miriam married to?"

"Miriam Yoder?"

"*Jah.*"

"She's an *alt maedel.*"

"What?" He hardly believed that. "Why? How? As beautiful as she is..."

Pete huffed, clearly losing patience with him.

"Listen, Mike. If you're planning on playing the field, leave the women in our community out of your game. Go back to your *Englisch* world."

Ach... "But she's single. Maybe she's looking for some fun." He cocked a brow.

"She isn't." Pete glowered at him.

"How do you know?"

"She's not like that."

Oh, but she was... "We used to...have a thing."

Pete shook his head. "The way I heard it, you had a *thing* with *every* girl in this district."

"*Nee*, not every." There had been a couple that he had absolutely no interest in or that he'd been closely related to.

"Why are you even back here, Mike?"

His eyes drifted in Miriam's direction. "I came to recover. Spend time with my *grossdawdi*."

"I meant *here*. At meeting." He frowned. "You are not planning on getting baptized."

"*Nee, Dawdi* insisted I come. I had no choice." Might as well make the most out of the situation.

"Well, then I suggest you pay attention to the sermons." Pete looked at him pointedly.

Michael's eyes wandered back to Miriam. "I'll be paying attention, alright."

"To. The. *Sermons*." Pete huffed.

"Jah, jah. The sermons." No doubt they would be directed at him. If Pete knew about his reputation, there's a good chance the entire Amish district did. But he wouldn't let the sermons faze him. He enjoyed his footloose and fancy-free lifestyle. And he wasn't about to give it up for the bishop or anybody else.

FIVE

"What did you think of what Minister Jake said?" *Dawdi* pinned him with a discerning gaze. Could he read his thoughts?

Ach, had he even heard what Minister Jake preached on? "Which part?" He swallowed, hoping *Dawdi* would throw him a line.

"The lust of the flesh?"

He mentally squirmed under *Dawdi's* scrutiny.

Michael shrugged nonchalantly, doing his best not to show his discomfort. "Interesting. Typical Amish sermon." Long. Boring. At least he'd had a pretty woman to stare at. To dream about. To—

"You weren't even listening, were you?"

Busted. "I heard some of it." He desperately tried to recall one of the verses he'd heard over and over again throughout his Amish upbringing that might apply to a sermon on the topic. "Love not the world...neither the things that are in the world. Uh...the lust of the flesh, the lust of the eyes, the pride of life are not of the Father." *Not too shabby*. He grinned.

"*Nee*, you left some out. *Love not the world, neither the things that are in the world. If any man love the world, the love of the Father is not in him. For all that is in the world, the lust of the flesh, the lust of the eyes, and the pride of life, is not of the Father, but of the world. And the world passeth away, and the lust thereof: but he that doeth the will of God abideth forever.*"

"See, *Dawdi*. I didn't even need to attend meeting today. I knew you'd give me a sermon when we got home," he said wryly.

Dawdi frowned at him, his disapproval crystal clear. "I will not tolerate disrespect in my home, *gross sohn* or no. Do you understand?"

Thoroughly chastised, he hung his head. "Sorry, *Dawdi*."

"It's *Der Herr* you need to apologize to."

"See, that's what I don't get. I mean, I know you believe all the stuff in that book, but is it even real? Isn't it just something that was written by men? To me, it seems like it was just written by some stick-in-the-mud who hated their life and doesn't want anyone else to have any fun either."

Dawdi's eyes widened and his mouth formed an O. "If that is what you think, we must not be reading the same book."

"What do you mean?"

"Jesus said He came that we might have abundant life. *Der Herr* gives good gifts to His *kinner*. As a matter of fact, every good gift comes from *Der Herr*."

"Maybe."

"There is no maybe. *Gott* is not a liar." *Dawdi* speared him with a demanding gaze. "The verses I *chust* quoted. What is it about them you disagree with?"

Michael shrugged. "I guess the part about not having love if you live in the world."

"So you think you have love in your heart?"

"*Jah*. I think so."

"Really? For who? These women that you've shared the marriage bed with—that you were not married to—how did you love them?"

Michael's eyes widened. How on earth did *Dawdi* know these details of his life? Had he heard the rumors among the *g'may*? He swallowed hard. "Well, I..." He huffed. "Look, I've never forced anyone. Never. They were willing."

"That wasn't my question. I'm sure the devil is

happy to provide all the sin and pleasure you desire. But that is temporary. Sooner or later, there are consequences that will have to be dealt with."

He didn't know if he liked his life being under a microscope, especially *Dawdi's*.

"How are you displaying love, Michael? Is it by giving a woman attention, leading her on, only to dump her like yesterday's garbage? Is it by satisfying your own fleshly desires? Is it by possibly fathering children out-of-wedlock?"

"I've never fathered any children."

"You're sure about that?"

Actually, he'd never stuck around long enough to find out. Besides, he'd always—well, *almost* always—taken measures to prevent that. "Not that I know of."

"Which means it is quite possible. How many women have you been with, Michael?"

He shook his head. This conversation was getting *way* too personal. "Let's just say a lot."

"So, in reality, you could have many *kinner* out there. *Kinner* without a *gut* father to lead them, that will likely be raised in a Godless home. Unless their mothers had the doctors destroy the *boppli* inside them."

"I..." He swallowed. He had no words. He'd never even considered...

"Think about your life, *sohn*. You *think* you are having fun. But it cannot be fun for the one who is paying for your irresponsible behavior." *Dawdi's* eyes shown with tears. "You need to learn what love is. Real love. Love is not doing as you please, fulfilling your own desires. Love is selfless. Love looks to the other person's needs. Love is giving of yourself for the good of another person and not expecting anything in return."

Thoroughly chastised—again, Michael dropped his head—again. "I don't even know how to do that. This is how I've always been. Even if I *wanted* to change, I wouldn't even know where to start."

Dawdi reached for his Bible. "Start with reading about Jesus. He is our greatest example of love."

Michael hesitated when *Dawdi* offered his Bible, but he took it out of respect. "I don't..."

"Just read about the life of Jesus. That's all I ask."

Michael nodded, because he didn't know how to say *no* to *Dawdi*.

Miriam closed her eyes and allowed herself to go back to a place she hadn't visited often. She pictured Michael, with his gorgeous...well, everything. There had been no flaw in Michael Eicher, as far as she could see. At least, not physically speaking.

He'd had a dazzling smile, eyes a girl could get lost in, and a build that could land him on the cover of a magazine. Of course, Miriam would never be that shallow as to think that looks were everything.

Nee, at first, she'd been reticent to agree to a ride with him. She'd seen him take many girls home in their district. Most of them, actually. But he didn't seem to be interested in any of those girls. As a matter of fact, she couldn't remember Michael taking any of them home more than a couple of times. With many of the girls he'd courted, it had only been once. Perhaps he'd known what he was looking for and none of them were it.

She didn't want to guess. She figured she'd be like every other girl. Ride home with him once, maybe twice, then he'd move on. Unless he decided she was the one for him.

So when he'd asked her home a third time, and beyond, she was sure they'd had something. Just knowing he'd escorted so many girls home had made her nervous. But after just ten minutes or so, he had set her mind at ease.

Michael had been a likeable guy, for sure and certain. His sense of humor, intense stare, and words of kindness were enough to make any girl fall for him.

And Miriam had. She'd fallen hard. After their third, then fourth, ride home together, she was certain he was the one. Her one and only.

Ach, she'd been so foolish. She took for granted that he'd meant every word he'd spoken to her. She'd certainly meant her own words. But he hadn't meant any of them. Not one. Every single word had been a bold-faced lie. Nothing more than bait to lure her into his arms. Like a snake charmer playing his *pungi*. And it had worked well. She'd given him everything, believing he'd be hers for always. He'd charmed her for sure and certain.

No doubt he'd laughed when attending his final gathering and he'd asked a different girl to ride home with him. He hadn't so much as looked her way. In fact, he'd ignored her completely. As though she didn't exist. She'd been thoroughly humiliated. And it had all been nothing more than a game to him.

Just a couple of weeks later, Michael had shaken the dust off his boots and left their community for good. And good riddance. She hoped she'd never have to see his face again.

She'd been so disgraced after what he'd done. She never returned to a young folks gathering after that. *Nee*, she'd left the community shortly thereafter and stayed away for nearly two years, allowing her battered heart to heal. But the *Englisch* life had not been for her. She'd missed the ways of her people. She'd missed her folks and her siblings.

But when she returned, things hadn't been the same. She joined the church, but she decided not to pursue a romantic relationship with anyone. It hurt too much to lay her heart out, only for it to be trampled on. She didn't think she could ever trust another man again. How would she know whether they were sincere in their affections toward her? She'd thought Michael had been. She'd been so so wrong.

Now, Michael was back home. And living in his *grossdawdi's* house, no less. Which meant she'd have to see him on a regular basis. Perhaps she should quit her job. But she'd been caring for Sammy Eicher for two years now and they'd formed a bond. She'd felt like he was kin now, like he was her own *grossdawdi*. They'd had many conversations.

He encouraged her to find a man, not knowing it had been his own *gross sohn* that had turned her against love. Sammy had been married over fifty years. Ever since Roberta—Bertie—died, Miriam had been the one to care for Sammy.

Her family had always been close to Bertie and Sammy. They'd been neighbors Miriam's entire life, living just three houses away. In fact, Bertie had watched over Miriam and her siblings a few times when her folks had traveled to other states for weddings and such. Most of Sammy and Bertie's relatives still lived in this community too, but Michael's family had moved back to Pennsylvania.

Michael hadn't grown up in this community, so they'd never attended school together. In fact, he and his immediate family had only been in the area for a couple of years before they'd met. When Michael left the community, his folks relocated shortly thereafter.

SIX

This was the day Miriam had been dreading. Ever since she'd learned of Michael's return, her heart had been tumultuous. But she couldn't let his presence interfere with her care of Sammy. If only Michael was more like his *grossdawdi*. Strong, faithful, trustworthy, upright. If only...

She quietly called through Sammy's screen door.

"Come on in, *maedel*."

She drew in a breath of courage and stepped into Sammy's house. "*Guten morgen*, Sammy."

"How's my favorite *maedel* doing today?"

Her gaze flitted around the quiet living room.

Sammy leaned close and whispered. "He's taking a nap. Said he was exhausted."

She nodded then shrugged. "I'm well in body. The other parts are quite *ferhoodled*."

"I think I might know why." His brows lifted and

he gestured toward a bedroom.

How did Sammy know? Was she that obvious? Or had Michael mentioned something? "It's not easy seeing him again."

"You two...?"

"A long time ago. It's ancient history now."

Sammy nodded.

"What would you like me to do?"

"Would you mind starting with the dishes? I'm afraid I've gotten behind." He shook his head. "My *gross sohn* can't do too much yet with his broken arm."

And she knew how much Sammy's arthritis bothered him. He'd likely not been able to do much more than prepare their meals. She made a mental note to prepare extra dishes and stick them in the freezer for future use. Perhaps she'd make a breakfast casserole for them.

"What injuries does he have?"

"He had some pretty *gut* scrapes and bruises. The doctor's main concern was a concussion he had, but that seems to be fine now. *Chust* a broken arm and a broken leg. *Der Herr* spared his life for sure. I hope this will be a wake-up call for him."

Wake-up call or not, Miriam planned to keep her distance.

"Oh, and before you start, would you mind

fetching the dishes from Michael's room? I don't think he'll wake up. He's on some strong medication that knocks him out."

She swallowed. "I...I can do that." So much for keeping her distance.

Sammy stepped out onto the porch, while Miriam filled the sink with hot soapy water. She inhaled slowly, holding her breath for a few seconds, then exhaled. She could do this.

She tiptoed to the door of the spare bedroom and turned the knob as quietly as possible. Good. Just as Sammy had said, Michael seemed to be out like a light, a soft snore escaping his perfect lips. Why had she noticed his lips? Her eyes inadvertently roamed over him as he slept. *Ach*, he was just as handsome as he'd always been, if not more so. One of his tan muscled arms rested at his side, while the other lay across his bare chest in a cast. His chest rose and fell with each breath he took. He was so attractive she could hardly look away.

She mentally chastised herself, remembering why she'd entered the room in the first place. Great. His dishes were on a table. On the *other* side of the bed. If she went around the bed, she might bump it and wake Michael up—the last thing she wanted to do. But she didn't want to reach over him either. Perhaps Sammy would forgive her if she washed Michael's dishes later? But no, he'd specifically asked her to retrieve them.

Quit being a coward!

She gathered her resolve and opted for the latter option. As gingerly as possible, she reached over the bed. Glass in hand, she startled when something brushed up against her chest. She looked down to see Michael's hand.

Horrified, she took the half-filled water glass and splashed it in his face. Then seemingly of its own accord, her hand flew across his stubbled cheek. "Don't you *ever* do that again!"

She stormed out of the room empty-handed. From now on, Michael Eicher would fetch his own dishes. And as far as she was concerned, he could wash them too. Injured or not.

She was quite certain Sammy would side with her on this one. *Ugh!*

Michael smirked as Miriam stomped off. He'd always liked her spunk. But boy did she have an arm! He rubbed his cheek, which was likely bright pink. Too bad she couldn't have slapped the side that hadn't been bruised in the accident. It now throbbed.

He knew he'd deserved it, though. That and more.

He didn't know what had come over him, except that he woke up to this beautiful form hovering over him. He could hardly help himself. It seemed like the perfect moment. A dream come true. He'd definitely been dreaming about her.

He hoisted himself from the bed and reached for his crutch. Time to deal with damage control. He grasped his dirty dishes, tucked them in the crook of his cast, and hobbled toward the kitchen. When he came to the entrance, he stopped dead in his tracks.

Miriam stood in front of the sink, her backside facing him. He eyed her lovely form, with curves in all the right places, and stifled a groan. Pure perfection, to his thinking.

And right off the bat, he'd blown his chances with her. *Idiot*. It would be twice as difficult to get into her good graces now. He shook his head, frustrated with himself. He'd never been prized for his wisdom.

"Hey." He hoped she'd turn around. He attempted his most gentle tone. "About what just happened...I'm sorry, Miri."

She continued with her dishes, completely ignoring him.

He hobbled closer and set his dishes on the counter next to her.

"You can wash those yourself." Well, at least she'd

spoken to him. Not exactly the words he longed to hear, but it was better than the silent treatment.

"I might need some assistance." He admitted sheepishly.

"*Jah, vell,* you'll not get it from me."

"Come on, Miri. I said I was sorry."

"*Jah,* you're sorry alright. Now, if you'd leave me in peace, I'd appreciate it. I have a job to do."

He sighed. Okay, he'd leave her alone. For now.

Miriam fumed so intensely, she wondered if she had actual steam raging from her ears. Of all the nerve. Michael Eicher hadn't changed one bit. He was still the cocky, insincere, selfish jerk that had left the community five years ago.

And he'd had the audacity to call her Miri. He knew she'd always loved his nickname for her. How dare he use it to try to manipulate her into getting what he wanted. Well, it wouldn't work this time. She was no longer the naïve eighteen-year-old she'd been when they'd courted.

In spite of his irresistible smile and voice as smooth as molten dark chocolate, she would *not* fall for his charms again. She. Would. Not.

SEVEN

After *Dawdi* uttered the silent prayer and cleared his throat, Michael dug into the delicious supper Miriam had prepared for the two of them. The aromas had been tantalizing his senses all afternoon. As soon as the cheeseburger casserole hit his taste buds, he moaned.

"She is a *gut* cook, ain't so?"

"She's amazing." In so many ways. "How on earth is she not married?" He hadn't meant to utter that aloud in front of his *grossdawdi*, but he had nevertheless.

"I suppose she hasn't found the one *Der Herr* has planned for her. If He does have someone in mind for her."

"Any man would be lucky to have her as a *fraa*."

"Any man?"

He shrugged. "Well, any Amish man. I don't think she'd consider an *Englischer*."

"*Nee*. She would not." *Dawdi* wiped his mouth. "How did you two get along while I was out?"

Michael shook his head. "We didn't. She refused to speak to me."

"And why's that?"

"'Cause I'm stupid. And don't ask me to elaborate on that."

"No elaboration needed." *Dawdi* chuckled.

"Gee, thanks."

"So you *do* want to explain then?"

"No. Let's just leave it at that."

"Did you court Miriam in the past?"

He took a sip of his water. "I did."

"And?"

"And that was a long time ago. I don't think she'd give me the time of day now."

"Probably just as well. She is Amish. You are not anymore."

"How often does she come over?"

"A few times a week to help me out. But she checks in on me every day."

"Every day?"

"She likely worries about me being alone here. Probably won't stop by as often since you're back."

"That's too bad. I wouldn't mind seeing her every day."

"Why?"

"Have you seen her? She's the hottest Amish woman in this district. Probably in the state. Which is why it baffles me that she's unmarried."

"It's not because of lack of interest on the part of the young men." *Dawdi* eyed him carefully. "I've seen many an interested fellow look her way."

"Now, *that* I believe."

"Seems she's been deeply hurt. Doesn't trust easily." *Dawdi's* mien turned somber. "You wouldn't happen to know anything about that, would you?"

He swallowed. "I might."

"*Ach, sohn.* Consider your life. What type of legacy do you want to leave? If you would have died in that motorcycle accident, what do you think people would have said about you at your funeral? What would you want them to say? Or even more important, what will you say when you stand before *Der Herr*?"

"That's pretty morbid, *Dawdi*." He frowned.

"I want you to seriously think about it." *Dawdi* bowed his head for the closing meal prayer and Michael followed suit.

Michael pushed away from the table. "I'll put the food away and the dishes in to soak."

"I'm sure Miriam will appreciate that. *Denki*."

"He drives me absolutely crazy!" Miriam unloaded on her best friend.

Nora nodded. "What did he do?"

"You don't even *want* to know. And I don't even want to say it."

"That bad, huh?"

Miriam stomped her foot. "I don't know how I'm going to put up with him. Seriously. It's been one day and he's already stretched my last nerve thin."

"I think—"

"And it wouldn't be so bad if he wasn't so...so...gorgeous." She clenched her fists and closed her eyes. "Ugh...why can't his looks match his personality?"

"There once was a time you liked his personality."

"He was different then. At least, I *thought* he was." He'd been so sweet and attentive and caring. Wonderful, in fact. But it had all been a ruse. Some sick joke to him.

"He's a fake if I've ever seen one."

She pointed at Nora. "Don't ever let me fall for him again."

"You say that like there's a possibility of it." Nora's pointed look hit its mark.

"There isn't. But you know how persuasive he can be. If I'm around him day after day, he's going to try to wear down my defenses."

"Well, at least you recognize that. You're a lot wiser than you were back when he was courting you."

"About that..."

"You know what? He did that to every girl. You realize that, right? He only wanted one thing, and since he could wave his smiling wand and put an instant love spell on the girls, he probably got it more often than not."

"And I thought I'd broken the spell. Instead, he only held me under it longer. I was such a fool."

"No. *He's* the fool. He missed out on a good thing with you, Miriam. And you deserve someone who is going to love and cherish you. Don't ever settle for less."

"I don't know if I'll ever find that." The realization cut deep. Because, honestly, she longed for someone special. Someone who would cherish her for who she was. Someone who would love her. Her, not her looks or her body, but *her*. She abruptly turned and wiped away the pesky tear that escaped. She needed to rein in her emotions. No need to let her best friend see her cry.

"You will, if it is what *Gott* has planned for you. You can trust Him and His timing." Nora's eyes livened with mischief. "Who knows? Mr. Right could charge into town on a white stallion tomorrow and sweep you off your feet."

Miriam giggled. "You always know how to put me in a better mood."

"That's what friends are for, ain't so?"

"*Jah. Denki.*" She pulled her friend into an embrace before heading home for the evening. Who knew what tomorrow would hold?

EIGHT

Michael's gaze fixated on the words on the page. Although he'd heard these stories growing up, he never *really* considered that they might possibly be true. But...now? They were nothing short of amazing. He'd taken *Dawdi's* advice and began jotting down notes. He stared at the words in his notebook now.

The concept of God's love—of Jesus—baffled him. These people hated Him to the point of killing Him, yet He loved them anyway. Surely God, being who He is, knew this would happen to His Son. Surely Jesus knew as well. Yet, He came to earth anyway.

Moisture pricked his eyes unbidden. How...? Why...? He, above all people, was undeserving of this love, and he knew it. He'd messed up so badly, probably even more than he realized. He'd left Miri broken and hurt. So much so that she refused to speak to him. How could God just look past all the wrong he'd done and offer him forgiveness? It just didn't seem possible.

"Breakfast is ready, if you are." *Dawdi* called from the entrance to his room.

"*Jah*, okay. I'll be right there." He left his Bible on the desk and joined *Dawdi* in the kitchen.

As he sat there, staring off into space, he sensed *Dawdi's* eyes boring into him. "Everything all right?"

"*Jah*. I've been reading, taking your advice."

"And? Something you want to talk about?"

He blew out a breath. Might as well get this off is chest. If anyone could help him, *Dawdi* could. "God wouldn't ever forgive someone like me, would He? I've messed up too much. I've ruined lives. I've been a complete idiot."

"Have you tortured and killed an innocent person?"

"No, of course not."

"Well, do you remember what Christ told those who'd crucified Him?"

"*Jah*. Father, forgive them. For they know not what they do." He quoted by heart.

"Exactly. I think that if God can forgive those who nailed His Son to a tree, who caused Him extreme pain and rejected Him, then He has ample forgiveness for you too. His word says that if we confess our sins, He is faithful and just to forgive us our sins and to cleanse us from *all* unrighteousness."

"But how can He do that?"

Dawdi chuckled. "If you're asking me how *Der Herr's* mind works, I'm afraid I can't answer that. His thoughts are not my thoughts. I don't know how *Gott* works, I *chust* know He does. He desires fellowship with His creation. Sin stands in the way of our relationship with Him. If we receive His forgiveness, the barrier between us is removed and we can freely enjoy fellowship with Him."

Michael thought on *Dawdi's* words. It was interesting that the same thing that prevented his relationship with *Der Herr* was preventing his relationship with Miri. Perhaps if he fixed his relationship with God, his relationship with Miri would begin to heal as well.

"Do you think *Der Herr* can help me make things right with Miri?"

Dawdi smiled. "I believe He can."

He'd definitely be praying for it.

"Miri, can we talk?"

Miriam cringed just hearing Michael's voice.

"There's nothing to talk about."

"I think there is."

She took Sammy's shirt out of the wash basin and fed it through the double rollers. "I'm kind of working right now."

Michael moved near. He plunged his uninjured hand into the water and pulled up another shirt, then handed it to her.

She stared at him. "I don't need your help."

"I want to help. This is something I can actually do. You don't know what it's like being cooped up in my *grossdawdi's* house and not being able to do much of anything. I'm going crazy."

"I thought you were already crazy." Why was she teasing him? She shouldn't let him draw her into his net. She had to resist his charms.

"It's been said." And there was his million-dollar smile. The one she couldn't help but reciprocate.

She had to get rid of him. "Listen, I appreciate the help. But I can get this done quicker on my own."

"*Ach.*" He placed his good hand over his heart. "You wound me."

She rolled her eyes.

"Why is it that you're not married?"

She stopped what she was doing, shut off the agitator, then turned and walked out of the wash room.

"Miri, I'm serious."

Did he think she was actually going to respond to that? She ignored him and made a beeline for the house.

The sound of him hobbling behind her didn't escape her notice. Did he intend to follow her around all day? Because, if that was the case, she would have to quit coming over. This was something she could not, would not do.

"Will you please stop?" His voice sounded desperate. She didn't remember ever hearing anything but confidence in his tone in the past. Where was this coming from? Or was it part of his act?

She spun around. "What do you want from me?"

His eyes sparkled. "That is such a loaded question. A very dangerous one."

"You know what? Just stop. Stop following me around. I have work to do here."

"I will. After you talk to me. I promise."

"I know what your promises are worth." She retorted, continuing toward the house. Was there something she could do for Sammy that didn't include having a conversation with his grandson? She needed to find a room and lock herself in it. Or lock Michael out.

"Okay." He held up his one good hand. "I deserved

that. Forget I said promise. But will you please just let me have a few minutes of your time?"

"Why?"

"Tell me what to do. I want to fix what's wrong between us. I want to be your friend."

She squeezed her eyes shut. Boy, was he good at testing her patience. "I don't need a friend."

"Maybe I do."

"I can't be your friend, Michael."

"Why not?"

"You *know* why."

A burdened breath escaped his lips. "Miri, I messed up. Big time."

"*Jah*, you did."

"Can I have a do-over? Can we just forget about the past and start from scratch?"

Seriously?

"You're joking, right?" How on earth did he expect her to *just forget* about the past? It wasn't even a remote possibility.

"No, I'm not. I want to start over with you, Miri."

"Why?"

"Because I like you."

"No, Michael. You do not like me. You like yourself."

"Ouch. That's not a nice thing to say."

"It's the truth. You've only ever cared about yourself."

His face darkened and he frowned. "You know what? You are absolutely correct."

"You're admitting that you only care about yourself?"

"Yes. That was true in the past."

"In the past?" She refrained from snorting.

"Can we be friends? *Please*?"

"I can't just be friends with you, Michael."

"Then be more." He reached for her hand, but she yanked it away.

"No!" Her lashes prevented the wetness from rolling down her cheeks. "I'm *not* going to fall for this again. Just leave me alone, Michael." She flew out of the house. She might as well go home. There was nothing more she could do for Sammy today. Not with his grandson insisting on trailing her every move.

She headed down the road as quickly as her feet would reasonably carry her, without breaking into a jog.

"Where are you going?" Michael hollered after her.

"Home."

"What about the laundry? You left the washer full."

Arguing with him from a hundred yards away was

ridiculous. She glanced over her shoulder. "I'm sure you can figure out a way to finish it up. I'm leaving."

She left off in a sprint. By God's mercy, he wouldn't follow her home. She could only stand so much of Michael Eicher in one day. If only he'd go back to his *Englischer* world and stop terrorizing her heart.

Miriam pinned a dress to the clothesline while stewing as she thought about her day at Sammy's. She felt terrible about leaving the laundry undone, but she needed to retain her sanity. And doing that with Michael at her side seemed like an impossibility.

The creaking of buggy wheels and horse hooves drew her attention. The rig belonged to Sammy. Oh, no. If it was Michael...

"Hello." Sammy's friendly face peeked from the side of the buggy.

Miriam sighed in relief when she discovered he'd come alone. "Hi, Sammy."

His smile disappeared. He gestured to *Mamm's* bench that graced the edge of her garden. "*Kumm, maedel.* Let's talk about what is on your mind."

She left the remaining clothes in the basket and joined him in the garden. "I'm having a hard time, Sammy."

"Because of *mei gross sohn, ain't so*? He's been bothering you?"

"*Jah*."

"I can find somebody else to help me out if you wish, although I'd miss you terribly."

Miriam covered his aged hand with hers. "I won't leave you, Sammy. Even if I have to put up with Michael."

"He told me you two used to be sweethearts?" His brow lifted slightly.

"It is something I regret. I thought he loved me. But it turned out that he only loves himself. I know that sounds harsh, but it's the truth of the matter. I...I would have married him if we'd stayed together. But then he left..." And her world was turned upside down.

"I am sorry, Miriam." Sadness filled his features. "Have you prayed for him?'

Sammy's words hit her like a brick in the face. Shame filled her. No, she hadn't prayed for him. Not really. At least, not a heartfelt prayer. She'd been too upset. It hadn't even entered her mind to *really* pray for Michael, actually.

She shook her head. "*Nee*."

"Maybe it's time to start then."

"*Jah*. I will."

"And I will assign my *gross sohn* extra chores when you come over. He can drive the buggy yet, so I will send him on errands when I can."

"I would appreciate that, Sammy."

"He hasn't tried to..." Sammy shook his head and sighed.

The last thing she wanted was for Sammy to be worried about her wellbeing. He didn't need added stress in his life. "It's nothing I couldn't handle. I'm fine. I just had to get away from him today."

"You let me know if he bothers you again. I plan to go home and have a stern talk with him. He should respect your wishes."

"Thank you, Sammy."

NINE

Michael yawned as he rose from the bed. The scent of *Dawdi's* savory sausage had woken him out of his sleep. Good for him, today was an off-church Sunday. Miri hadn't so much as glanced his way at the last meeting. He'd barely seen glimpses of her over the past few weeks. He had no one but himself to thank for that. He shouldn't have come on so strong the first week he'd been here.

He had just a couple more weeks until his casts could be removed and it couldn't happen soon enough. Hardly being able to do anything had been trying his patience. He wanted to use all of his members. It had been so long since he'd gone for a jog—something he loved doing. His muscles were likely to be flabby after neglecting the gym these past weeks.

He couldn't wait to get back to his normal routine.

Not that it would be normal. He'd decided to stay with *Dawdi* for a while. Maybe he could lessen some of Miri's work load. Hopefully, he'd be able to secure a job once he had his strength and movement back. He needed income. The bills had begun pouring in from the hospital. He'd have to start making payments on them soon.

He knew *Dawdi* would help out if he needed him to. But he was a grown man. He'd pay for his own bills. He wouldn't be any more of a burden to his *grossdawdi*, if he could help it.

"We are having company over today." *Dawdi* set breakfast on the table just as he entered the kitchen.

Michael removed two plates from the cupboard and set them next to their forks and steaming coffee mugs. "Who?"

His *grossdawdi* took his place at the head of the table and they bowed for the silent prayer. "Peter Stoltzfus and his family. You two used to be friends, ain't so?"

"*Jah*. Used to be." Pete hadn't been too friendly toward him since he'd been back. Of course, he'd been eyeing his friend's wife his first time back at church. If *he* were married to Miri, he'd probably be upset if another man had his sights set on her. *Whoa! Where did that come from?*

Marriage? He'd never really considered it for himself. He'd been an avowed bachelor. Always thought marriage was for boring people with boring lives. Not that Miri would ever give him the time of day. He'd pretty much blown that chance. If there ever was one.

"What time are they coming over?"

"About ten, he said." *Dawdi* sipped his coffee. "I'd like you to help with something after breakfast, if you would."

"Sure. What?"

"I bought a swing. I want to put it up."

"A swing?"

"For the *kinner*."

"I think Pete only has one old enough for a swing. The other one is still a baby."

"*Jah*. I know. *Chust* wanted to have something for the little one."

"Sure, *Dawdi*. Just point me in the right direction."

"I plan to hang it on the large sycamore tree out front."

"Sounds like a good place."

Michael flipped the steaks on the grill with his uninjured arm.

"Those smell great." Pete grinned as he pushed his little boy on the swing Michael and *Dawdi* had hung earlier.

"They've been marinating for a couple of hours. Should be nice and juicy." Michael raised his eyebrows twice.

"Can't wait." He nodded. "Hey, what are your plans?"

"Don't know exactly. I'm itching—literally—to get these casts off. I hope to find a job. The hospital bills aren't going to pay themselves."

"*Jah*. That can be rough."

He grimaced. "Over twenty grand. Who has that kind of money?"

"Not me." Pete chuckled. "No insurance?"

"Nope. I did have insurance on my bike, though. They're going to replace it."

"Oh, man. I miss my motorcycle. Do you remember it?"

"Sure do. That's why I ended up getting one. I always thought they were cool." He grinned like a fool. "The women like them too. Well, it seems most *Englisch* women do, anyway."

Pete nodded and quickly changed the subject. "If the insurance replaces it, at least then you'll have transportation, right?"

He shrugged. "I don't really have anywhere to go right now. I'll probably be better off if I just take the money and put it toward my hospital bills."

"So you're going to stay with your *grossdawdi* for a while then?"

"That's the plan."

"*Gut*. I like having you around."

That had been a shock to hear. "You do?"

"You've mellowed out since you've been here."

"I'm not sure everyone would agree with that statement." He chuckled.

"Have you thought about settling down?"

"I..." He shook his head. "I don't know about that."

"There are blessings to be had, brother. There's nothing like holding your own flesh and blood in your arms. Having a good woman who will stand beside you through thick and thin. Owning your own place."

Michael nodded slowly.

"It's something to consider, anyhow." Pete shrugged.

"You don't regret it? I mean, being tied down to one woman and all?"

Pete snorted. "Not for a minute. Sandy Mae and these kinner are the best thing that's ever happened to me."

"This little one's ready for her daddy." Sandy Mae, who'd been inside helping *Dawdi* ready the drinks, came near and handed their infant daughter off to Pete. "And you..." She moved to the boy on the swing and tickled him. "I think it's time for you to wash up. Dinner's about ready."

Their son moved close and looked up at Michael, his eyes wide. "What are you making?"

"Steaks."

"Can I see 'em?"

"Sure." Michael realized that the boy was too short. Pete's son reached his arms out to him. He'd never really held many children. "You want me to pick you up?"

The boy nodded, his eyes alive with excitement.

"Okay. I've only got one good arm, so you'll have to hold on." He lifted the boy, who didn't seem to weigh much more than a sack of feed.

"Do I get my own?"

"That's up to your dad."

"They smell really good."

"They do, don't they? I hope they taste good too." Michael smiled. He let the boy down, then took a plate from *Dawdi* and placed the steaks on it. "Let's eat!"

The entire afternoon, Michael couldn't get over

how much he enjoyed Pete and his family's company. Here he had been expecting to be bored out of his mind.

Except...Pete's life didn't seem boring. It seemed fulfilled. With one woman. And children. How could that be?

Michael stared after Pete and his family in wonder as they drove away. How could they possess such contentment? Why was it *he* was living the life he wanted, yet he was unfulfilled? Where was the joy that should have accompanied his chosen lifestyle? It was conspicuously missing.

Who did he even have? A few *Englisch* friends who probably didn't care where he ended up. And his *grossdawdi*, of course. But other than that, he really had no one who genuinely cared. His life seemed so empty.

His heart felt heavy all of a sudden. His gut twisted. His eyes burned.

He wanted what Pete had.

TEN

Michael had been contemplating the best way to approach Miri. He'd scared her off last time, which resulted in not seeing her for a couple of weeks. His *grossdawdi* had asked him not to bother her, and he agreed that he wouldn't. At least, he'd try. But if they didn't talk, they'd never be able to work through any of their problems, which he desperately wanted to do. They needed to clear the air. To start fresh. Except, Miri said she wasn't willing to the last time they'd spoken. Which presented an obstacle.

Hopefully, if he caught her while she was feeding the chickens, she'd be too distracted to remember that she didn't want to have anything to do with him. Yeah, that was hoping against hope, but he had to at least try. Because, if there was *any* chance he could possibly have something with Miri like his friend Pete had with his wife, it would be a dream come true.

It was peculiar how much his attitude had changed since spending time with Pete. His single *Englisch* friends would think he was insane. Which, he probably was.

"Miri, will you give me a minute of your time?"

"We've been over this before. I thought you agreed to leave me be." He hated that he'd been the cause of the anxiety in her voice.

"I did, except..." He sighed. "Listen, I get it, Miri. I have been a horrible wicked person. I've done many bad things, terrible things. I know. I realize what I am, who I've been. But I don't want to be that person anymore. I don't want that life."

Miri huffed. "If your words meant something to me, I might just believe you. But they don't. *I* don't. You've done a wonderful job of proving what your words are worth and I see it clearly now, Michael. You will say and do *anything* to get your way."

"But don't you see? That's not who I am now. It's not who I want to be. I want to change."

She shook her head. "Again, those are just words."

"Well, then what on earth can I do to get you to change your mind?"

"Honestly, I have no idea." She turned and abruptly walked out of the barn.

76

Michael shouted a curse word and punched one of the stall posts.

"If you're trying to impress her, that's likely not the best way to do it." *Grossdawdi*. He stepped out of a shadowy. stall

"I'm sorry, *Dawdi*. But she is impossible. Nothing I do is good enough for her. She has completely written me off." He ignored the blood dripping from his knuckles.

Dawdi moved close to Michael and placed a hand on his shoulder. "The trouble is, you're trying to do something only *Der Herr* can do."

"What's that?"

"Do you *really* think *you* have the power to change another person's heart? *Nee*, you don't possess that power. Only *Der Herr* can do that. I suggest you step out of the way and let *Gott* do His own work in her heart."

"I don't know if I can. I mean, I wouldn't even know where to start."

"Start with prayer, *sohn*."

"Prayer?"

"Pour your heart out to *Gott*. He will listen. Ask in faith, believing. The prayer spoken in faith can move mountains."

"But what if that mountain isn't meant to be

moved? What if I pray for her and she still doesn't want me? What if it isn't *Der Herr's* will?"

He nodded. "May be. But I suspect there is a reason neither of you are hitched yet." His brow rose upward.

"Do you...*really*? Do you really think there's a chance for us?" It was the first shred of hope he'd had and he would cling to it with all his might. If his *grossdawdi* thought they might have a chance, then it could just be possible. His heart soared.

"I'm afraid you've got it all wrong. Your life is not about pursuing or pleasing a woman, or any other human being, for that matter. Your life is about pleasing *Gott*. At the end of your days, it will be between you and *Der Herr*. No one else. Do not worry about the other things, trust *Der Herr* to take care of those things for you. You *chust* serve Him."

"But I want Miri so bad—" He snapped his mouth shut at *Dawdi's* frown.

"Seek ye *first* the kingdom of *Gott* and *His* righteousness, and all these things shall be added unto you."

And there it was.

It was like a light finally clicked on in his head. Or the lantern had finally been lit, to put it in Amish terms. And everything around Michael seemed to brighten. He'd been missing it. All this time. *Ach*, how much time he'd wasted! He'd chased everything *except* God.

But now he knew. *Now* he had the golden key that unlocked every door. Or as *Dawdi* had put it *"all these things"*. Was it really that simple?

As though *Dawdi* had read his thoughts, he murmured, "You must surrender. Totally surrender your life to *Der Herr*."

Michael nodded and determined from that moment on that he would surrender. He bowed his head. *God, please forgive me. Help me to live the life You have for me. And please let Miri see me for who I am in You. Amen.*

"Paul said, *I die daily*. You must ask for *Der Herr's* strength for each day."

"I will do that." He raised his head and stared at his grandfather. "*Dawdi*, I think I'd like to rejoin the g'may."

"*Gut*." Tears misted *Dawdi's* eyes. "*Sehr gut, sohn*."

And in that moment, Michael knew that with God holding the reins, he could go anywhere, accomplish anything. Even his pursuit of securing the perfect wife.

It was time to get on his knees. Now, if only he could kneel.

ELEVEN

Having Michael back in the community had been challenging at best. To admit the truth, Miriam had been confused by his actions and his words. Was she wrong in not giving Michael another chance? Was she wrong to guard her heart so fiercely? She hadn't thought so, but maybe...

"*Kumm, maedel.*" Sammy patted the empty space next to him on the couch. "Tell me what is on your mind. I can see that you carry many burdens."

Miriam frowned. She glanced around the room.

"If you're worried about my *gross sohn*, he is not here. He has gone to the hardware store and will not be back for a while."

She put her dusting rag away and joined her elderly friend on the couch. "I don't know...I don't know if I should share this. I've never told anyone."

"Well, it is up to you, child. But I know that getting

things off one's chest can help bring peace and healing. And you know you don't have to worry about me telling a soul."

She sighed. "Do you remember how I told you about when I left? When I was out in the *Englisch* world?"

He nodded in silence.

"Well...I'd made some mistakes."

"We all make mistakes. That is why we need a Saviour, to forgive our wrongs." He gently placed his weathered hand over hers. "Have you sought forgiveness?"

"Many times."

"You need only ask once. *Der Herr* is not hard of hearing."

"*Jah*, I know. I just don't *feel* forgiven."

"That is called guilt. Let *Der Herr* have your guilt, Miriam."

"I've tried. I just can't seem to forget." As a matter of fact, she'd thought of little else. Especially since Michael's return.

"*Der Herr* loves you. He wants you to have the peace that passes all understanding."

"I have no idea how to get that."

"You must trust in *Gott*. He will place peace in your heart." He stroked his long white beard. "You have no power to change the past. It will always be there. The good, the bad, all of it. It isn't going anywhere. But you don't have to dwell on it. You have the power to forgive yourself and move on. You have the power to choose to trust. You will never find contentment if you hold on to what will never be or what could have been. *Der Herr* can give you a *wunderbaar* future, but only if you'll allow Him to. You will first have to let go of the past. You will need to believe *Der Herr* has forgiven you—not because you *feel* it, but because He promised He would. And *Der Herr* keeps His promises. Do you believe that?"

She shrugged. "*Jah*. I mean, I want to, but..."

"But what?"

"Sammy, have you ever felt like *Gott* wasn't there? Like you prayed to Him, but He didn't answer?"

"I have felt that way, for certain sure. But I realized something. My ways and my wants are not always what *Der Herr* wants. He knows what is best." He looked at her and frowned. "Do you remember the story about the footprints?"

She nodded. "The Footprints in the Sand?"

"*Jah*. Remember the time when the man could only see one set of footprints? Then he realized that *Der Herr* had carried him? *Chust* because we do not see *Gott*, it doesn't mean He is not with us."

"I didn't feel like it when I was in the *Englisch* world. I felt all alone."

"Yet, you are back here in your Plain community. That makes me think that maybe *Der Herr* was with you, guiding you. He brought you back home, ain't so?"

"*Jah*, he did."

"You suffered many things in the *Englisch* world, ain't so?"

She nodded slowly. "I lost so much..." Tears surfaced, but she didn't wipe them away.

"You know what my Bertie used to call me?"

"*Nee*."

"The best secret keeper. If you need to talk, if you want to, I am here to listen. What you say will stay between the two of us."

"I..." She pulled in a breath. *Ach*, it would feel *gut* to have someone to tell her secrets to. "Before I left...well, me and a boy, we...we made a *boppli*." The tears spilled over her lashes and slid down her cheeks.

"An *Englisch* boy?"

Her fingers twisted in her lap. "*Nee*. Amish."

He frowned with his entire face, his own sorrow at the realization likely matching her own. "My *gross sohn*, ain't so?"

"How did you know?"

"I have seen how he's lived his life. I'm afraid my *gross sohn* has never been known for his wisdom."

Nee, he was known for his *gut* looks. His fast life. His rebellion.

"And what happened?"

"I knew Michael wouldn't be coming back to the Plain life. He was seeking fun. Adventure. Another life. He wasn't ready to settle down. I still don't think he's ready." She brushed away the wetness from her face. "And I wasn't ready. I was too ashamed to raise a *boppli* on my own. I was ashamed to face everybody—my family, the *g'may*."

"Where is the *boppli* now?"

"I gave him up for adoption to an *Englisch* couple who couldn't have a *boppli*."

She didn't miss the disappointment that briefly flashed across Sammy's face. But he attempted a smile. "I'm sure and certain you made them very happy."

"*Jah*, they were. I met them. They seemed kind."

"That is *gut*. But I'm guessing you miss the little one?"

"Not a day goes by that I do not think of him. I can't help but feel that he will think I abandoned him. I didn't. I just wanted him to have a better life than what I could have given him. I wanted him to have a complete family. A *mudder* and a *vatter* who love him. I wanted him to be happy. But, *jah*, my arms have ached to hold him many times. Then I realize that I will never hold him again." She sobbed. "A piece of me died the day I gave him up. I knew I could never be the same. That I would never know true happiness. But I knew it was best."

"*Ach*, Miriam." Tears shined in Sammy's eyes as well and he gripped her hand. "Does Michael know?"

"*Nee*. I have not told him. I didn't think he'd care."

"I think you should tell him. If anything, he needs to know the sorrow he has caused. He needs to know that his actions have consequences. That what he does has an effect on other people. That sin is not all fun and games."

"You must think that I am a bad person. Back then, I...I thought Michael and I would get married. I would have never..." She squeezed her eyes shut against the pain. *Ach*, she'd had years to get over this. This should all be behind her by now. But it wasn't. *Nee*, it felt like a fresh wound. Like it had just happened yesterday. "I was so foolish to believe his words."

"We have all been foolish at times. You have a right to believe a person is telling the truth when they speak. I am sorry my *gross sohn* lied to you and dishonored you."

"I loved him. I thought he'd loved me too. I don't understand what I did wrong." Fresh tears trailed her cheeks. "I don't know why he left me."

"I don't think it was anything you did. My *gross sohn* had his own *ferhoodled* ideas. He was irresponsible." Sammy embraced her briefly. "I will not disclose your secret. I won't tell him. But I really think *you* should."

TWELVE

"Hey." Michael stared after the Amish man behind the shop counter. He wasn't from his *grossdawdi's* district but he looked so familiar. "Silas Miller? Is that you?"

The man's head shot up. "*Jah.*" A quizzical look crossed his features.

"Mike Eicher. From Pennsylvania, remember? Joe Beachy and I were good friends." He thought about his friend Josiah and wondered how he was doing. What was he up to? Where did he live now? Had he gone back to the Amish?

"*Jah, jah.* I remember." A beautiful Amish woman with a baby in her arms and two children beside her came and stood close to Silas. "Meet *mei fraa*, Kayla. This is our *dochder*, Bailey. Our son, Judah." He ruffled the toddler's hair and leaned down to pick him up. "And our *boppli*, little Shiloh."

"Bailey, huh? I've never heard that as an Amish name. I like it."

"*Ach, mei fraa* was an *Englischer* before we married."

"Well, that explains it." He shifted from one foot to the other. "I didn't know you lived around here. I thought you were still out in Pennsylvania."

"My family moved when we were in *rumspringa*. Been here several years now. How about you?" The toddler in Silas's arms attempted to remove his hat. "*Nee*, Judah."

"I'm staying with *mei grossdawdi* right now."

"Wife? Kids?"

"No. None." Why did he feel so empty saying those words?

"*Ach*, that's too bad. Well, you never know what *Der Herr* might have planned. I never thought I'd marry an *Englischer*."

Yeah, Michael never would have imagined Silas married to an *Englischer* either. Yet, here he was.

"We own this store and the house out back." He thumbed over his shoulder. "You and your *grossdawdi* should stop by for supper sometime."

"Do you know my *grossdawdi*, Sammy?"

"*Ach*, Sammy Eicher? *Jah*, I know him well. I order feed for him quite often. And he loves Kayla's pot pies."

90

"Do you have any in stock? That would be a treat for him."

"Sure. They're just over in the refrigerated section. I think we might have a couple fresh ones left. If not, I can take some from the freezer. Kayla makes several at once and we take them out as needed."

"Do you have peanut butter spread?"

"Sure do. Aisle two."

"Great." He studied Silas. "Hey, you wouldn't happen to know of anyone who's hiring, would you?"

He watched as Silas's family exited and waved. "It was nice meeting you," Kayla said.

"You too." Michael waved to the little ones and their smiles brightened even more. He turned his attention back to Silas once his family stepped out the door.

"I know my *Dat's* always looking for *gut* help. He has a construction business." He eyed Michael's casted arm. "But that's not likely something you can do right now."

He never cared much for construction. "Nah, probably not."

"You can take a look at the bulletin board. Sometimes folks post stuff on there." He pointed near the door.

"Okay, I'll check it out."

"Are you Amish now?" Silas eyed his plain clothing.

"No." He looked down at his arm. "These injuries are from a motorcycle accident."

"I see." Silas nodded. "Do you own a car? Amish are always needing rides. Doesn't pay too much, but it's something."

"*Ach*, no, I don't." He scratched the stubble on his cheek. "I've actually been throwing around the idea of joining the church." He'd only mentioned that to one other person—*Dawdi*, but for some reason he felt at ease with Silas.

"Really? That's *gut* to hear. Would that be here or in Pennsylvania?"

"Oh, I have no plans to return to Pennsylvania. It would be in the same church as *mei grossdawdi*."

"*Gut, gut.*" Silas nodded. "No special *maed*, then?"

"One. But I've got my work cut out for me." He chuckled. That had been the understatement of the year.

"I understand that quite well."

"I can imagine."

"But it's definitely worth it. After my first *fraa* passed away, I never dreamed I'd have another family again. But *Der Herr* has been *gut* to me. He's given me things I never imagined I could have. I never thought I could ever be this happy. Not that we don't have problems. We do. But we get through those with *Gott's* grace and life goes on."

Michael frowned. His friend had already experienced *two* marriages? Wow. How was it that Pete and now Silas could be bound with a ball and chain and still possess such contentment? It went against what most of his *Englisch* friends' and coworkers' relationships had taught him. What was the difference?

I AM.

What on earth? Had that voice been audible? He glanced at Silas, who didn't seem to have heard it. Was he going crazy? He shook his head.

"Are you...okay, Mike?"

"Weird." He shook his head. "I think I'm hearing things."

His friend eyed him curiously.

"Never mind."

Silas chuckled. "You're not alone, friend."

"What do you mean?"

"I've heard a voice too."

"What did it say?"

He leaned over the counter. "Not it. He. It was *Der Herr*."

Hadn't he been thinking the same thing?

"And?"

"And I ended up marrying Kayla because of it. But I was reading *Gott's* Word. It was like the words jumped right off the page and into my heart."

"Whoa. How did that happen?"

"I don't know, except that it was a spiritual thing. I knew it was *Gott* talking to me. I had no doubt. What he asked of me seemed impossible. I just wanted to follow Him. To show His love to Kayla and Bailey. He showed me exactly how to do that. And I have great peace because I know I am living in His will."

"Wow. That's nothing short of amazing."

"I don't know what you're looking for, Mike. But just know that it can be found in *Der Herr*."

"You're sure?"

"Absolutely." Silas rubbed his beard. "Isn't it something that we both came from Pennsylvania and ended up here in neighboring districts in Indiana?"

"Quite a coincidence, I'd say."

"Oh, it's no coincidence. I believe *Der Herr* orchestrates these things."

"It would seem so." Michael thought on it for a moment, then held out his good hand for Silas to shake. "Thank you for your words. I needed to hear them today."

Silas nodded. "I wish you well, my friend."

THIRTEEN

Nora's gaze zeroed in on Miriam, as though she was contemplating something, but Miriam couldn't decipher her mood. Surely her friend was tiring of hearing her go on and on about her woes concerning Michael Eicher. "You said he mentioned joining the *g'may*?"

"Yes. Well, Sammy said he planned to join."

"That's...interesting." She nodded slowly.

"Not really. He'd been baptized before he ever came here. He was shunned in his Pennsylvania church. I don't think he takes *any* vow seriously."

Nora stared at her straight on. "Okay. I know this is going to sound strange, crazy even, coming from me."

Miriam's forehead creased. "What are you talking about?"

"What if he's sincere?"

Miriam snorted. "You don't really think—"

"Just hear me out." She held up a hand to stop Miriam's impending protest. "What *if* it's real this time? What if he actually means what he says? And he's here to stay?"

Miriam shook her head. She didn't buy it.

"I know you don't believe him. But I've been watching him at meeting. His eyes aren't roaming around searching for women like in the past. Except maybe a glance in *your* direction every now and then. He's been paying attention to the sermons as though he's interested in what the ministers are saying. When we sing, I've seen him close his eyes, as though he means the words coming from his lips. Miriam, there *might* actually be something to this."

"I don't know, Nora."

"Okay, so just say that he really *is* sincere. And he asks to court you."

"No." Miriam shook her head several times. "I can't."

"Why?"

"I just can't."

"Okay, I get that he broke your heart. But it's possible that he's finally growing up."

Broke her heart? *Nee*, he'd done much more than that. What she'd shown on the outside was just a sliver of the anguish she'd endured. It wasn't just a broken heart. It was so much more. It was the death of a dream. "I'll *never* date Michael again."

"So you're fine with him finding someone else then? Because if he sees that there's no chance with you, he'll likely give up. He's eventually *going* to settle down with a wife and have a family. And, as charming as he is, I don't suspect he'll have *any* difficulty finding someone."

No, he wouldn't. Not with his good looks.

"Good for him." Miriam said the words, but truthfully, they slashed her wounded soul even more. To see someone else with the life she'd wished for some years ago would surely make her miserable. But she couldn't fathom *ever* trusting Michael Eicher again.

❦

"*Dawdi*, I need your help. Your advice."

His *grossdawdi* smiled. "Now, that's something I never expected to hear from you."

"*Jah*, it's finally come to that." He jested.

"*Ach*, you must be desperate."

"I am. I've tried everything to get Miri back but she doesn't want anything to do with me."

"Can you blame her?"

"*Nee*, I cannot. I've been foolish."

"Well, at least you're willing to admit it now. That's something."

"Thanks, *Dawdi*." He said wryly.

"Pride will bring us low every time. We must seek humility."

Michael nodded. "I'm...trying."

"You will never be able to accomplish anything on your own. You must become intimate with *Der Herr*."

Michael frowned. "How do I do that?"

"Bathe yourself in His Word. Let the words wash over you and cleanse you from the inside out."

"I have been reading, but I don't understand how that will help me with Miriam."

"*Ach*, I will let you in on a secret. When you become like Jesus, you will be irresistible to a woman seeking a Godly man."

"I will?" A slow grin crept across his lips.

"Without a doubt."

"But...how long will that take?"

"Are you on a time schedule?" *Dawdi's* brow rose.

He shrugged. "I guess not. But I don't want to wait until we're *grosseldre*. No offense."

Dawdi chuckled. "I'm happy about my age. I'm that much closer to Heaven."

"You know what I mean. I don't want to waste time that we could be together."

"That's the first thing that will need to change."

"What do you mean?" He scratched the irritating scruff on his face. He needed to shave again.

"If you think spending time getting to know *Der Herr* is a waste, you're starting off on the wrong foot. *Der Herr* brings the greatest joy into my life. I cherish the moments spent in His Word." *Dawdi* pointed to him. "You need to change your attitude. Pray that *Der Herr* will come inside and teach you how to think, what to think. Make your thoughts obedient to Him."

"*Ach*, that sounds like a lot of work. Impossible even."

Dawdi nodded. "*Jah*. But with *Gott* all things are possible."

"How can you be so sure?"

"He's done it for me. He can for you too."

Michael scoffed. "I doubt you've had thoughts that rival mine."

"You've likely never thought anything I haven't already, *bu*. I'm ashamed to say that I've had many wicked thoughts in my lifetime. Still struggle some days. But *Gott's* grace is sufficient for me *and* for you. His strength is made perfect in weakness."

Wow. He didn't even know what to say about his *grossdawdi's* admission. Surely his grandfather's mind didn't go to places he sometimes allowed his thoughts to go. Did it?

"Where...? What do I need to do? I don't even have a clue where to start."

"Start with prayer. Ask *Gott* to show you, to open your eyes and your heart to His truth." He handed his Bible to him. "Just read."

"Will you show me your favorite verses? I mean, if we struggle with the same problems, there's a good chance the verses will be relevant to me too."

"They will be easy to find. I have my favorites marked."

FOURTEEN

$\mathcal{M}$iriam had been in Sammy's house washing dishes when a vehicle pulled up, spewing dust in every direction. Someone must've been in a hurry.

She dried her hands, prepared to meet the strangers—a man and a woman—but stopped when she reached the screen door. Michael had ambled out of the barn and went to greet them.

"Are you Mike Eicher?" Miriam heard the man ask.

Michael responded with a nod.

Miriam then watched as Michael and the man entered the barn. The woman stood just outside the barn's entrance.

Michael eyed the irate man warily. Hatred oozed off this man's body. It was so strong, he could almost ingest it. This was *not* going to go over well.

"My wife says you two had an affair!" *That explained it.* The man's hands balled into fists.

Whoa. He took a deep breath. He should have guessed that his past would eventually come back to haunt him.

Michael glanced at the woman. She did look like someone he'd brought home one time. "Your *wife*?"

"She said you *knew* she was married."

He rubbed the back of his neck. "I...uh...listen. If she wasn't looking for something, she probably shouldn't have been in a bar flirting with me and leading me on."

Perhaps that had been the *wrong* thing to say. Maybe the man would go easy on him since he still wore a cast on his arm and one of his legs. One could only hope.

"Of all the nerve." He looked him over and chuckled wryly. "Looks like I'm not the first one to get to you, you pathetic..."

Michael only understood some of the curse words the angry husband spewed as his fist connected with Michael's jaw, snapping his neck backwards. As if that hadn't been enough, the second blow to his stomach knocked him off his feet. He hadn't even had a chance to defend himself with his good arm.

"That was a warning. Next time, I won't be so kind and gentle. Don't you *ever* even think of coming near my wife again!" The man grabbed his wife's elbow and pulled her back to the vehicle.

Michael released an excruciating sigh of relief when he heard the motor start and the tires heading in the opposite direction of Dawdi's property. He attempted to breathe normally but his body wasn't having it. Had one of his ribs been dislocated? Or cracked? He hoped not. After dealing with these casts the last five weeks, he was anxious to have them removed. He didn't need another one. At this rate, he'd never be able to work a job.

He heard footsteps and glanced up. *Oh, no. Miri.*

"Michael, who was..." She stopped speaking when she spotted him sprawled out on the barn floor. "What happened? Are you okay?"

She rushed over to him. Her fingers feathered over his bleeding lip. Having her touch him was almost worth the pain he'd endured.

"*Jah*, I feel like a million dollars," he jested.

She shook her head and frowned in disapproval. "Can you stand up?"

"I don't know." He grimaced as he attempted to sit up. He hugged his middle with his good arm. "Ahh! I think one of my ribs might be busted." He panted.

She gasped. "I'll go call a driver to take you to the hospital."

"Miri, no." He reached out his good hand. "Please. I don't want to make my *grossdawdi* worry. Besides, I already have enough to pay with my hospital bills from the accident. Will you please just help me up? Help me into the house."

"Michael..." She was about to protest, then reluctantly nodded. "Okay." She crouched next to him and slipped her arm behind his back. "On the count of three, we're going to stand up."

"Three." He nodded, holding his breath in anticipation of the pain.

"Put your arm around me."

"I thought you'd never ask." He teased in spite of his agony.

She attempted to frown at him, but he knew she fought a grin. "Do you *ever* stop joking?"

He shook his head. "How fun would life be then?"

"Ready? One. Two. Three." She grasped his arm with her other hand and carefully pulled him to a standing position.

He immediately grabbed onto one of the barn poles, breathing heavily.

"Are you all right?"

"I'll be fine. I just need a minute." He inhaled

several more labored breaths.

"Would it be better if I ran to the house and got your crutch?"

"I don't think so. If you'll just help me walk to the house." Besides, he wanted her near.

"Okay."

She gripped his waist and his good arm tightened around her. He hobbled to the house as best as he could, wincing with each step. If it wasn't so agonizing, he'd be enjoying this a whole lot more.

"Are you all right?"

"I'll get through it."

She opened the screen door. "Where do you want to go?"

"The bedroom." He added a hint of suggestiveness to his voice just to ignite her ire. He loved seeing the beautiful blush on her cheeks when he teased her.

Her brow shot up faster than a gunman's draw in the Wild West.

He cleared his throat. "To rest and hopefully put something on this," he clarified. *Although...*

"Would you rather have something hot or cold on it?"

"My face or my ribs?"

"Both."

He gently lowered himself onto the bed. "Ice will

be great for my busted lip. I think maybe something hot might soothe my ribs."

"I'll go get something. Can you take off your shirt?"

"This *must* be my lucky day." He couldn't help his smile. Or his teasing.

Miri just shook her head.

"Truthfully, I think I'm going to need help. If you would?"

She nodded slowly, then sat next to him on the bed.

His heart pounded hard at Miri's closeness. He swallowed as her deft fingers worked to unbutton his blood-stained shirt. Had her hand brushed against his chest on purpose, or was it just wishful thinking on his part? He was probably delirious. If only she'd lean a little closer and brush his lips with hers. He shook the thought off and attempted to assist her by sliding his arm through the sleeve. He needed to get his act together. He couldn't ruin this.

Her face filled with horror. "Oh, Michael! You look terrible."

"Not exactly the reaction a man hopes for when removing his shirt for a lady." He chuckled but it ended in a wince.

"Look at that bruise. It must hurt like crazy."

"*Jah*, it does. But I suppose I deserved it."

"You mind telling me what happened?"

"Jealous husband." He grimaced.

She frowned with her whole face, then promptly stood from the bed.

He was tempted to reach for her. "Look, Miri. I wasn't the perfect saint out in the *Englisch* world."

She rolled her eyes. "Like you've *ever* been the perfect saint."

"Ouch. That wasn't nice."

"Would you rather I lie?"

"Lie? No. But a little flattery goes a long way."

"I'm not into flattery. You should know that by now. People only use flattery when they want something from you."

"See, Miri, that's what I like about you. You hate my guts but you still helped me."

A hurt look flashed across her face. "I don't hate you."

"Really? Hmm...you won't talk to me. You don't want to be my friend..." He shrugged. "Seems like it."

"I'm talking to you now, aren't I?"

"Only because it's the cordial thing to do."

"I'll go get your ice pack." She fled from the room like her hair had caught fire.

Jah, he'd blown it. Again.

FIFTEEN

This cannot be happening. Miriam berated herself. How could Michael Eicher still have such an effect on her? She'd been trying *so hard* to ignore him, to build up an immunity to his charms, but she clearly was not inoculated yet. She was beginning to believe there was no cure. That the undoing of her heart was inevitable. Either that or he possessed some sort of unseen power over her thoughts and emotions.

Why couldn't this catastrophe have happened when Sammy was here instead of her? Not that she wanted Sammy to see his *gross sohn* in such a state. Or add extra stress to his life. Okay, so maybe it was a better idea for her to be present during that whole ordeal than Sammy.

Ugh.

Maybe she should just march over to Michael and

tell him how it was going to be. She would tell him, in no uncertain terms, that she would never, *ever* let him court her again. That she wasn't interested in him. That she wasn't attracted to him in the least.

But that would be a lie. Of course she was attracted to Michael Eicher. Who wouldn't be? But that didn't mean she had to fall head-over-heels for him every time he was around. She knew, probably better than anybody in this district, what he was like. Both the good and the bad. And the bad was enough for her to steer clear of him. But she couldn't do that right now. No, he had to go and get himself beaten.

Ugh.

"Miri?" Michael's strained voice called from the other room. "Do you have that hot pack yet? My ribs are killing me."

She swallowed. "*Jah.* I'll be there in a minute."

There was no time to dwell on her volatile emotions at present. A patient needed tending to. And right now, she was the only one who could be a nurse to him.

She entered the bedroom with an icepack in one hand and a hot towel in the other. "Here, put his on your lip."

He winced as he held the icepack to his face. "Oo...it's cold."

She quickly looked away after realizing she'd been staring at his toned arm. "Don't be a baby."

She glanced down at the hot towel in her hand. *Great*, she should have given this one to him first so he could put it on his ribs. Now, she'd have to be the one to do it.

Michael looked up and seemed to read the indecision in her eyes. "Don't be a baby." He playfully repeated her words.

"I..." She huffed, frustrated that he'd rattled her. "Fine."

He was enjoying this attention way too much.

She could do this. She folded the steaming towel in half and gently placed it over his bruised ribs, doing her best not to notice the gentle curves defining his chest or the way his abdomen flexed when she'd come near. *Ach*, he looked better now than he had five years ago, if that were even possible. He must've been working out at one of those fancy gyms when he'd been out in the *Englisch* world, because she was quite certain he hadn't been lifting bales of hay.

"Aah!" he hollered.

Fortunately, she'd been yanked out of her improper thoughts and quickly pulled back. "Are you okay?"

His grin spread across his face. "I was teasing."

She planted a hand on her hip and shook her head. "You know, I should really leave and let you handle this by yourself. You seem to be doing just fine."

"Come on, Miri. I'm just trying to find humor in a painful situation here. If it makes you feel better, it really does hurt. Badly."

"You're taking advantage of me."

"Maybe. But I need you." His voice had softened. "In more ways than one."

"Michael..."

"Please? Just give us another chance. Just one more. If I screw it up this time, I won't ever ask again. Miri, I want to start over with you."

"*Nee*."

Her conversation with Nora flashed through her mind. *What if he's sincere?*

❧

Michael prayed inwardly. *Please, God.* "Tell me why."

"Why? There are a thousand reasons. But let's just start with one. I could never trust you again."

"But...I'm different now, Miri. I've decided to join the church." He reasoned.

"Vows mean *nothing* to you." She stared at him hard.

"I admit that *used* to be the case, but like I said, I've changed."

"I'm sorry, Michael. I wish I could believe you. But I don't."

"Why? Do you not believe a person can change?"

"*Nee*, I do. I just don't believe *you* have changed."

"I don't know what I can do to convince you." He felt like weeping. "I'm *trying* here, Miri! I want to begin a relationship with you. I want you as *mei fraa*." Did he sound as desperate as he felt?

She closed her eyes and shook her head. "It's too late for that."

He dared to reach out and touch her hand. "*Nee*, it's not too late. You are still single and so am I."

"So you want to marry me...again? Like last time, ain't so?" She tugged her hand away.

"No. *Not* like last time." A weight settled on his heart and pressed down hard. *Ach*, he'd shredded every ounce of trust Miri had. He didn't know how he would get it back. "I admit it that I didn't mean those words back then. I only wanted one thing and I would do just about anything to get it. I was wrong, Miri. I didn't deserve you.

"The truth, Miri, is that I began to care for you in ways I couldn't understand. But I wasn't anywhere near the settling down stage yet. And I guess part of me was scared. I wasn't ready to assume a full-fledged Amish life with all its rules and responsibilities. When

I realized that, I stopped taking you home from the gatherings. I thought if I began seeing someone else, I wouldn't think of you anymore. It didn't work. That's when I decided I needed to leave the community altogether."

"*Jah*, but then you became *Englisch* and had *fancy* women, ain't so?"

He prayed she'd never find out how many. How he wished he could go back and erase those years, that time in his life, all his foolish decisions. But he couldn't. That was who he was then. "*Jah*," he sighed. "I did."

"But if you *truly* cared for me, you would not have done that."

"It's hard to explain. Before I began courting you, I'd already...well, I'd given myself away. More than once. It created this desire inside me that could not be quenched. It became like an addiction. I had to have it." He hung his head. "If there was anything I could change in my past, that would be it. But there is nothing I can do about it now."

"And I'm to believe you will be happily married to one woman after you've shared the marriage bed with many? *Nee*, I'd be even more foolish than last time. I'd have a husband who would deem me inadequate. A husband who would compare me to every other woman he'd been with and leave me, to seek fulfillment elsewhere. A husband that would leave me to raise a houseful of *kinner* alone and that I'd never be able to get away from because we do not believe in divorce. *Nee*, I won't do it."

"But I've changed, Miri! For real. I wish to God that you would believe me. Won't you please give me another chance? I promise I will not be any of those things. That is not the life I seek anymore."

"What if I'm not enough for you? I cannot be married to a man who desires other women. I won't do it, Michael. I'd rather remain an *alt maedel* my entire life than have to deal with an unfaithful husband. I just couldn't bear it." Tears pricked her eyes. "It crushed me when you left last time."

"I really am sorry about that, Miri. And truthfully, you will *never* be enough for me. But *Der Herr* is enough. He is enough for you. He is enough for me. Whatever happens, it is *Der Herr* who will be there constantly. He promises to never leave us or forsake us."

"I think you should move on. Without me. Find someone else. Maybe that will be enough for someone else, but it just isn't for me."

"Someone else? There is no someone else."

"Well, there is no *me* either. I'm sorry, Michael."

"Why? Just tell me why you don't believe I can change. Am I beyond God's power?" He fought back the tears that welled in his eyes.

She stared at him, as though searching his soul, as though grasping for a thread of truth in his words. She shook her head. "When you left our people, were you aware that I left too?"

"*Jah*, someone...my *grossdawdi*, I think, mentioned that you'd left for a time."

A tear slipped beneath her eyelash, trailing her cheek, then another. She brushed them away with shaky hands. "Nobody knew. I was in the *familye* way. I carried your *sohn*, our *sohn*, for nine months. I lived among strangers, *Englischers*, until I had him." She shook her head and forced away another avalanche of wetness with her dress sleeve. "I wanted to keep him. I longed to...I wanted so much to have a happy family, a husband who would love me and our *boppli* more than anyone in the world. But I realized that would never happen. *Nee*, he'd only grow up in shame and humiliation when he realized what kind of *vatter* and *mudder* he had. I did not want that for him, so I gave him up—hoping, praying, that he would grow up in a home with love. Not a day goes by that I don't think of him, wonder how he's doing. Is he happy? Does he feel loved? Have his adopted parents told him he'd been born to someone else?"

His jaw dropped at her revelation. He had a son? *They* had a son? His mouth opened, then closed again. *Ach*, what could he say to that? What a *dummkopp* he'd been!

"I..." He shrugged, not having a clue what to say. She'd been right. Even if he'd known about it then, he wouldn't have had the maturity to properly father a child. "*Ach*, Miri. I'm so sorry."

He dared to touch her shoulder, longing to hold her. To somehow help ease her sorrow.

She jerked away. "Don't! Just don't!"

His gaze trailed her as she ran from the room. He felt completely helpless just lying there in this bed. He couldn't even run after her. His own eyes stung with unshed tears as he realized the enormity of it all. No wonder she hated him! He'd been the most selfish person alive. He'd fulfilled his lust then left her with a gaping hole in her heart, still bleeding till this day.

He bowed his head and whispered a prayer. "God, please help! I need You. I cannot fix this on my own. You are the only one who can heal Miri's heart."

His heart sank into his stomach. This wasn't an acceptable outcome. Somehow, he'd prove to her that she could trust him—that in spite of everything that had happened, they could still make it work. He had no idea how, but he was determined to make it a reality. Now more than ever.

⁂

Dawdi walked into Michael's bedroom, just as he'd shifted, groaning loudly. "Want to talk about it?"

"This?" He pointed to his face. "Just my past coming back to haunt me, is all. I guess I shouldn't be surprised." He shrugged.

Dawdi eyed his swollen lip and put two and two together. "I'm afraid the law of sowing and reaping doesn't just go away, even after you've given your heart to *Der Herr*."

"Apparently not. I deserved this and more."

"Do you need a doctor?" *Dawdi's* brow furrowed in concern.

"I figured I'd just wait until I go in to have my casts removed. I can ask then if it's still bothering me." By the pain he was experiencing now, he knew it would be.

"What is wrong?"

"Mostly my ribs. Although I'm not sure if they are dislocated, cracked, or just bruised." He grimaced as he pulled in a breath.

"You could see my chiropractor. He should be able to tell."

"Is he open today?"

"I think probably."

"Great. Let's make an appointment then."

Michael had never been so thankful for chiropractors in his life. The doctor correctly guessed that his rib had likely only been dislocated. After a quick x-ray to assure that his assumptions were correct and it hadn't been cracked, he made an adjustment—which had been excruciating at the time—but seemed to have done miracles. Although Michael was still bruised, he could now breathe easily and his pain had greatly subsided.

Michael felt like giving the chiropractor a hug, but he refrained. He'd bet money that he hadn't been the first patient to have that thought, though. He guessed some probably had indeed hugged the man. The miracle worker.

Now, to get his casts removed next week. Things were looking up.

SIXTEEN

Michael had been pondering the situation with Miri since their conversation the other day. At least now all their cards were on the table and they knew the truth. That was something. But where should he go from here? Miri had stated, rather clearly, that she had no intentions of ever getting back together.

It seemed hopeless. But he was not one to give up easily when he saw something he wanted. And he wanted a real relationship with Miri more than he'd ever wanted anything in his life.

But the question was, *how* did he go about pursuing that relationship?

Michael moved his arm around in a circle several times, thankful to have the use of it again. It had felt a little stiff since his cast had been removed, but he didn't let that stop him. The doctor had told him to use it as much as comfortably possible to get his full range of motion back. He walked with a limp, but the doctor had assured that his leg would get stronger each day. He was just glad he was now able to take a normal shower. Since his casts had to stay dry, he'd had to use plastic bags and rubber bands to ensure moisture wouldn't enter them, which had been extremely inconvenient and caused his showers to take twice as long. It was funny how having an injury involuntarily taught one not to take normal things for granted.

He'd finally be able to go out job hunting and hopefully get on his feet in more ways than one.

"*Dawdi*, do you ever feel like you just want to throw in the towel? Just give it all up and do something completely reckless?" he asked.

"Can't say I do. *Der Herr* has taught me contentment."

"Well, I do."

"Seems to me you've already tried that before. Didn't work out too well, by my thinking."

"You're right." He gritted his teeth. "Sometimes, I just hate myself. I am so stupid."

"You have made unwise decisions, that is true. But you are far from *dumm*."

"But I *am*. Look at my life." He lifted his hands and

twisted in a half circle. "Miri can't stand the sight of me. Everyone else my age has their life together. A wife. Kids. They own their own home and provide a decent living. I can't even keep a job for more than a few months. I'm so far behind I don't know if I can ever catch up."

"They who compare themselves among themselves are not wise."

Michael frowned. "What are you saying, *Dawdi*?"

"You need to focus on pleasing *Der Herr*, not anyone else. Live for an audience of One."

"But every time I—"

"There are no buts. Don't make excuses. Excuses are for the weak. Be strong in the Lord and in the power of *His* might. There is nothing you *can't* do if Christ is your strength."

Michael shot up from the bed. That had been some dream. A *wonderful* dream, in fact. Could the scenario even be possible? *Dawdi* had said, with God *all* things were possible, right? And now he was with God and God was with him.

Just like that, he *knew* what to do. Without a doubt. For the first time in his life, confidence flooded his soul. *No*, his entire being.

There was no mistaking, *Der Herr* had given him that dream.

❧

"Sammy? Do you know where Michael is? His room is empty and I didn't see him anywhere outside. Did he go into town?"

Sammy frowned. "I don't know. He was gone when I got up this morning." He slid a piece of paper across the table. "Left this note."

Her eyes scanned the words.

Dawdi,

I'm sorry I left without saying goodbye, but I have an urgent matter to attend to. I can't explain anything right now. I don't know how long I'll be gone. It could be a while, I don't know. Please don't worry about me. Thank you for all you've done. And please keep praying for me.

Michael
P.S. Tell Miri I'll make this up to her.

Miriam turned the paper over and frowned. "That's it?"

"I'm afraid so."

"Where did he go? What urgent matter is he referring to?"

Sammy shrugged. "Wish I could say."

"He didn't talk to you?"

"No. I had no idea until I found that. Last time I talked to him, though, he said he felt like doing something reckless." Discouragement blanketed Sammy's face. "I guess he won't be joining the *g'may* after all."

She knew it. This was *so* typical of Michael. Just when she was beginning to trust him, to open up her heart. Moisture burned her eyes. "I'm sorry, Sammy. I...I have to go."

She turned and ran out of the house, allowing the tears to fall freely. How could she have been so foolish? She should have known better. She should have seen this coming. Michael hadn't changed. He was the same selfish jerk he'd always been. Why had she believed any different?

SEVENTEEN

Michael tapped his fingers on the desk as he waited for someone to pick up on the other end of the line. He really shouldn't have sprung for a hotel, but he needed privacy and this was likely where he'd be able to acquire some. Since his cell phone had been damaged in the motorcycle accident, the only phone he'd had access to was the phone shanty. He couldn't chance anyone in the *g'may* finding out about his business, so he'd opted for this.

He blew out a breath when someone finally answered. "Hello. I need to know how I can get information about a baby that was put up for adoption about four and a half years ago."

There was a pause on the other end of the line. "What kind of information are you looking for, sir?"

"Who he was adopted by. Where he lives now."

"And who am I speaking with?"

"My name is Michael Eicher. The baby's biological father." He squeezed his eyes shut, shunning the tears that threatened. To think that he actually had a son. And with Miri, of all people.

"I'm sorry, sir, but that information is classified."

His heart plunged into the pit of his stomach. "Don't I have any rights as a biological parent of the child?"

"Sir, if your child was given up for adoption, you no longer have any rights."

But... "I didn't even know about the pregnancy. I had no idea she'd had a baby."

"I'm sorry, I don't think I can help you. When your child was offered up for adoption, your parental rights would have been terminated."

"Even if I didn't know?" This didn't make any sense to his thinking. "Wouldn't I have had to sign something?"

"Not if you couldn't be located or if you weren't named as the father."

"What do you mean?"

"If a woman states that the father's identity is 'unknown' or if the proper channels have been implemented to locate the father and they have failed, there is something called 'involuntary termination of parental rights' whether you personally agreed or not."

"That's absurd! So I can't even see him? Like *ever*?"

"I'm afraid adoptions are sealed cases. We look after the child's best interest and I'm not sure that would be in the best interest of the child. Besides, if it was a closed adoption, there's nothing you can do until the child turns eighteen."

"Eighteen?" He couldn't help his raised voice. Neither could he fathom waiting to see his son until he was eighteen. *Wait*. "But you said *if* it was closed. Is there a possibility it wasn't?"

"It's not probable, but yes, it is possible."

"And if it's *not* closed?"

"Then there *might* be options."

Michael nodded. "Okay. Options. That's great." He rubbed his hands together. "How can I find out?"

"If you're in contact with the birth mother, you could ask her."

He thought on the situation. Could he derive that information from Miri without her suspecting something? "And what if I can't get the information that way?"

"We will have to do some investigating into the matter and then get back to you. But you'll probably need to prove your paternity before we can proceed."

"How do I do that?"

"You take a test to see if your DNA matches. It does take some time and there are costs involved."

He frowned. "So if the adoption is open, what does that mean as far as being able to see my child?"

"Since your paternity has not been established yet, it means nothing. However, if it's an open adoption, there's a good chance the birth mother is allowed to have contact with the adoptive parents. But that's only if it's open."

"The birth mother. Okay, I'll see what I can find out." He grimaced. "We're not exactly on the best terms right now." Why had he said that out loud? It wasn't like it was anyone's business.

The other end of the line was silent.

He cleared his throat. "Will you give me your name so I can call you back if I have any more questions? I might need to do the paternity test thing if I can't get the answers I need. Also, what time does your office usually close?"

"My name's Brenda and I'm usually in the office till five, Monday through Friday. If I'm not in, you can always leave a message and I can get back to you."

"Great. Thank you. You don't know how much I appreciate this." He quickly jotted down her information, double checking to be sure he'd written everything correctly.

He hung up the receiver and blew out a noisy breath. Time for the difficult part—talking to Miri. Perhaps he should take advantage of the quiet motel room and spend some time in prayer. Because if he ever needed strength and courage, it was now.

Michael held the reins in one hand, attempting to rid the clamminess of his other hand on his trousers, then proceeded to do the same thing with his alternate one. If Miri didn't agree to go for a ride with him, he'd have to wait until she came to his *grossdawdi's* house next. But then, they might not have privacy. A buggy ride was a sure way the two of them could be alone. The only problem was that Miri's family or anyone else might misconstrue this as a date. Which was fine with him, but he was certain that Miri would have a problem with it.

He stopped at the Yoders' hitching post and hopped down from the buggy. He walked to the side door, the typical entrance the family used, with a confidence he certainly didn't feel. He glanced down at his *for gut* clothes and knocked on the door.

The door sprung open with a whoosh, and Miri's younger brother stood before him. The boy's eyes sparkled with mischief as his chocolate-covered lips told on him.

Michael smiled. "Will you get Miri—uh, Miriam—for me?"

"Mir-i-am!" The boy hollered at the top of his lungs. "There's a boy here to take you courtin'!" The boy spun on his heel and rushed back inside.

"No. I just want to speak with her." Michael called after the boy just as the door closed in his face.

Ach, this wasn't going well so far. He heard noises inside the house, but couldn't decipher what was going on. A moment later, the door opened again. This time it was Miri.

Her eyes widened. "Michael? What are you...I thought you left."

"I just needed to find some answers. Um, can we talk?"

She carefully studied his clothing, then eyed his buggy. Something akin to distrust crossed her face. She sighed. "Michael..."

"This isn't a date, Miri, I promise. Unless you want it to be. I just need to talk with you." He lowered his voice. "And it's something that can't be said with others around. Will you walk with me? Please?"

EIGHTEEN

For the life of her, Miriam wished Michael Eicher wasn't so pleasing to the eyes. With him dressed in his Sunday clothes and the scent of something rugged and masculine caressing her senses, denying him was nearly impossible. Add that to his natural good looks and she could hardly resist. Five years ago, she would have thought she was the luckiest girl alive to have Michael show up on her doorstep, but now?

"No." The word automatically popped out of her mouth.

"Miriam." He stuffed his hands in his pockets, then glanced toward one of the windows. He leaned close to her ear and whispered, shooting sparks up her spine. "This is really important."

She'd never seen Michael Eicher so intense, so serious. She nodded. "Okay. Maybe just for a little bit."

"Do you mind...uh...taking a ride with me? I think we will be out of earshot if we're alone in my buggy."

She didn't want to think of herself alone with Michael in his buggy. The last time they'd ridden together... "Michael...I don't know...I don't think I can do this."

"I promise not to touch you or try anything. *Please*."

Her heart rate accelerated and she glanced at his buggy. It was just a buggy ride. Just to talk. Not a date. No courting. There would be no cuddling close, no passion under the stars, no goodnight kiss. Just a ride.

"Okay." She acquiesced.

He blew out a long breath. "Thank you."

True to his word, he didn't touch her, not even offering a hand to help her into the carriage. She waited for him to unhitch the horse from the post, then he hopped into the buggy also. She scooted as far to the edge as she possibly could.

He frowned. "Miri, you don't have to do that."

Yes, for her own state of mind, she did. His cologne, though not terribly strong, was enough to overwhelm her senses. It brought back too many memories, both good and bad. "I'm fine. What did you want to talk about?"

He chuckled lightly. "Down to business already, huh?"

She raised a brow and crossed her arms. "You said you wanted to talk. It's the *only* reason I am in this buggy. If you have something else in mind, you can let me off right here and I can walk back home."

Hurt flashed across his features. "Miri..." His lips smashed together. "I want to know about our *boppli*."

He glanced her way.

Their *boppli*. Their *sohn*. The one she'd thought about every single day since she'd learned she was in the *familye* way. She couldn't keep her chin from trembling. "Why?"

"Because you've told me next to nothing. I want to know about him. It was a boy, right?"

She nodded, cursing the moisture barely contained by her eyelashes. "*Jah*."

"When was he born? When is his birthday?"

"Why do you want to know?"

"It's my son, Miriam. You at least got to see him, to hold him. I never had that chance."

"They sent you a letter."

"What letter?"

"To let you know about the *boppli*. Papers to sign for the adoption."

His lips turned down. "I never received any papers."

"That is what I figured. Because I'm sure you

would have signed them, to give the baby up, if you had, *ain't so*? Since you didn't return the papers in a timely manner, they just put on there that you couldn't be found."

"So that was it? Even though it was my son too, they didn't even care?" His grip tightened on the reins, accentuating the veins in his hands.

"They said if you cared, you would have been there for me and supported me throughout the pregnancy."

"I cannot support what I don't know about." The bitter words flew from his mouth.

"Would you have, though?"

"I don't know." He shook his head. "But it would have been nice to have the option to decide for myself."

She cringed at the frustration in his voice. "I didn't know what to do, Michael. You left. I had no idea where you went. I asked around. I was scared and alone. I couldn't tell anybody about it."

"This whole thing is just so messed up."

"It's not my fault!" She couldn't keep her tears at bay anymore.

"Miri…" He reached over to cover her hand, then drew back at the last second. "I know it's not your fault. I'm not blaming you. I'm upset but not at you. I'm mad at myself and how stupid I was back then. I had everything. A beautiful girl, a baby on the way. And what did I do? I ran away like a coward."

She tentatively reached over and lightly covered his hand for only a second. "We were both *dumm*. I let my fear and pride and selfishness get in the way of caring for our *boppli*. I was more worried about what other people would think than what our baby will think. What kind of a mother am I?" The sob broke out unbidden.

Michael quickly guided the horse to the edge of the seldom-traveled country road. "Shh..." He scooted over and she allowed him to gather her in his arms. He gentled his tone. "Miri, it's okay. You were young. You did what you felt was best for our child."

Her tears drenched the shirt's fabric near his shoulder, but he allowed her to grieve as long as she needed.

"I've thought of him every day. Every day, Michael! What does he look like? What is he doing? Does he miss me? I used to talk to him every day when he was inside me. I have a feeling babies remember those things."

With the pads of his thumbs, he smoothed away the moisture on her face. His glance dipped to her lips momentarily, then flickered with something akin to desire. He immediately forced himself over to his own side, and looked off in the distance before bringing his attention back to her. He swallowed. "You...you said you met the people who adopted him, right? Was...was it an open adoption or a closed one?"

She'd never once seen Michael Eicher vulnerable. *Ach*, it was almost endearing. Nora's words flashed in her mind once again, *maybe he's sincere*. She shook off the thought as quickly as it had come.

"It was open, but I asked her not to contact me."

"Did you ever contact her?"

"I had planned to. I just didn't know what to say. And she couldn't have responded. If she did, then someone—maybe *Dat*, might get the letter and read it. I couldn't chance him finding out."

"But you still can, right? You can contact them?" Was he really serious?

She nodded, her hands trembling. Just the thought of contacting their *boppli's* adoptive parents made her nervous and excited all at the same time. "I have the papers locked away in my bureau. I bought a special box and keep it hidden in a drawer."

"How would you feel if we tried to contact them? We could ask about how he's doing. We can put my name and *Dawdi's* address on the envelope and no one but us and *Dawdi* would know."

She swallowed. "You...you would *want* to do that?"

He nodded then reached over and squeezed her hand. "Yes, very much. I'm sure they probably have pictures they could send. It would almost be like seeing him."

Tears resurfaced in her eyes. "You're sure?" *Ach*, it felt so *gut* to finally have someone on her side, someone to share her heartbreak and joy.

"I'm positive, Miri." He flashed his million-dollar smile.

Miri found herself slowly falling for him all over again. But she couldn't allow herself that luxury. As excited as she was about the possibility of seeing their *boppli*, she had to remind herself who she was dealing with.

Michael Eicher—the heartbreaker.

NINETEEN

Michael would never doubt the power of prayer again. He was certain the night he spent praying at the motel had paved the way for Miri's favorable response. It had gone far better than he could ever have hoped for. Not only had he discovered the adoption was an open one, but she was interested in contacting their baby's adoptive family.

And then...what had happened next was as close to a miracle as he'd ever seen. Miri had let him hold her in his arms. No, it hadn't been long. But it had happened when he thought there was zero chance of it ever happening again. She'd barely agreed to the buggy ride. *Ach*, he'd been *so* tempted to feather a kiss across her brow, to dip his head slightly and indulge in the softness of her lips. But he'd refrained. He couldn't scare her off again. He needed to learn patience—something he'd never possessed an abundance of.

"*Ach*, I see you've finally come in."

He glanced up at his *grossdawdi*, drenched in sweat from head to toe. He needed a bath. "I have."

"You are finished mucking out all the stalls, cleaning the chicken coop, stacking the hay, fixing the harnesses, washing the carriage, *and* feeding all the animals?"

"Yep. And I weeded the garden."

Dawdi chuckled. "My bones are gonna get lazy at this rate. By the look of things, I would think she let you kiss her."

"You would think so, wouldn't you?" He couldn't wipe the permanent smile off his face if he tried. "I can't help it, *Dawdi*. I've never felt so optimistic in my life! I feel like I could run a marathon and still have energy to expend."

"Speaking of energy—"

"Did the mail come?"

"*Ach*, calm down, *bu*. It's only been two days since you two sent off that letter. They have to receive it, read it, then write back. You may be waiting a while."

"I hope it doesn't take too long. I'm about to burst."

"Remember, *sohn*, *Der Herr's* timing is perfect."

"*Jah*, I'm trying to."

It almost seemed like she was the character inside a book, with herself and a couple of close confidants, harboring this deep dark secret that nobody could know about or it would spell the demise of their entire universe. Was she being overly dramatic? Probably.

But the scenario was partly true. She *did* have a secret that she'd kept hidden from everyone until lately. The revealing of her secret wouldn't necessarily cause her demise, but she'd most definitely be looked down upon. Thankfully, neither Sammy nor Michael had been condemning. Never in a million years had she ever dreamed of telling Michael her secret—now *their* secret.

She released a noisy whoosh of air. *Michael.*

He seemed...different somehow. Like he'd changed overnight. *Nee*, it wasn't overnight. Now that she thought about it, it had been gradual. First, the motorcycle accident had knocked his world out of orbit. She guessed that spending his recovery time with his wise old *grossdawdi* wasn't hurting him any. He'd been attending church regularly. And she'd spied a Bible on his nightstand.

Had *Der Herr* been working in his heart? Or was this all just part of his act to get her into his good graces so he could take what he wanted and leave her high and dry? Again.

Ach, she hoped the former was true. Because if it wasn't, she didn't think she'd ever be able to forgive Michael Eicher or herself again.

They'd been talking, having real conversations. About God. About life. About their *boppli*. He wanted a relationship, one he claimed would be permanent. But...was *anything* permanent with Michael Eicher? Judging from his track record, she'd have to say no.

However, she *did* recognize that *Der Herr* was all-powerful. He was the Potter who molded each vessel whichever way He wanted it. But sometimes the clay refused to yield under His skillful hands and ended up with divots and flaws. Then the Potter would have to begin all over again, and work the clay until it became a vessel He could use. Is that what He was doing with Michael? With her?

Michael had promised to contact Miri the moment the letter arrived. But he hadn't been expecting *this*. He stared down at the envelope in his hands and frowned. What could this mean?

He quickly stuffed it into his vest pocket and rapped his knuckles on the Yoders' door, hoping Miri would be the one to answer.

Instead, her little brother stared back at him—this time with what looked like flour or powdered sugar covering his lips and part of his forehead—with an insuppressible grin on his face. "Miriam! Your boyfriend is here again!"

"*Nee*, I'm not—" He'd attempt to prevent the boy from hollering out—again, but his efforts were futile—again. He hoped Miri wouldn't be embarrassed, but he guessed she was likely used to her mischievous brother's ways.

Instead of closing the door, though, the boy stared up at him. "When are you going to marry *mei schweschder*?"

A blast of heat zoomed up his neck when he spotted Miri behind her little brother.

She appeared flustered as she scooted around him. "Benny, *geh*!"

She quickly closed the door, but not before her brother started singing. "Miriam and Michael sittin' in a tree, k-i-s-s-i-n-g..."

He'd only uttered the first line before the door was shut, but Michael recalled the lines well.

First comes love. Then comes marriage. Then comes the baby in the baby carriage.

As they walked toward his buggy, Michael wanted to say something. But it would have to wait until others were out of earshot. Miri had kept quiet, and he deduced she was probably having an internal conversation, as was he.

Once they were on the road, he glanced her way. "I think we kind of went about that in the wrong order."

She turned to him and her brow shot up. "Huh?"

"The song your *bruder* was singing. We did that in the wrong order."

"*Jah.*"

"And I don't think I ever kissed you in a tree," he teased.

"*Nee.*" She seemed unusually quiet.

"You all right?"

She shrugged. "Just thinking."

"Want to expound on that?"

"*Nee.*"

"Okay." He fished the envelope out of his vest and handed it to her.

She took it, then frowned up at him. "This is *our* letter. Return to Sender?"

"*Jah.*"

"Maybe this is a sign that we aren't supposed to

contact them. Do you think?"

He shook his head. "*Nee*. It's just an obstacle the devil is putting in our path. Nothing *Der Herr* can't help us get around. They probably moved and it's been too long to forward it." At least, he *hoped* that's what it was.

"I don't have another address for them." Worry manifested in her tone. "How will we find out what it is?"

"We can go to the library and search on the computer. We'll find their new address that way." He could have said "I" instead of "we," but he wanted Miri to be involved in every step of this process. Every moment spent with her was a gift from God. One he vowed to never take for granted again.

"But what if they moved far away?"

He reached over and squeezed her hand. "We'll do what it takes."

"*Jah*, we will." A determined lilt gracing her voice was music to his ears.

They *would* eventually find their son. They would accomplish this goal. And they would do it *together*.

TWENTY

Michael stared blankly at the library's computer screen. Concentrating on the task at hand proved difficult with Miri hovering close by in the seat next to him. Her thigh accidentally brushed his more than once, setting his nerves on fire with each occurrence. The fruity-floral fragrance of her shampoo tantalized his nostrils. His senses were on overload with her nearness.

She pulled out the slip of paper, although she hadn't needed to. "Here are the names." Her whisper tickled his ear, teasing him, taunting him. Did she have *any* idea the effect she had on him?

He glanced at her, seeing that her eyes were trained on the screen. *Nee*, she had no idea. He cleared his throat. "Uh, *jah*. Milton and Sarah James." He quickly typed in the names.

As he scrolled down the screen, he clicked on a link

touting personal records. "This looks like a good one."

Miri nodded, tucking in her lips when he hovered over a name.

"Do you know how old they were?"

She shrugged. "Maybe in their forties?"

"Okay. This might be him." He clicked on a Milton James. He glanced at Miri. "There's a death date here."

"Oh, no. Do you think...?" Her words trailed off.

"I'll see if there's an obituary. If there is, it may have a photo." He clicked back to one of the previous screens, scrolled down, then clicked on a link. "Here it is. Does that look like him?"

Her hand flew to her mouth and she nodded. "*Ach, jah.* That's him."

Michael quickly scanned the article. "Survived by wife, Sarah, and son, Michael."

Her mouth dropped open and she stared at him in wonder. "Michael? They named him Michael?"

"Did you...did you tell them my name?"

"The lawyers knew, so maybe they said something to them? But, no. I didn't mention you at all."

They stared at each other for several seconds before he spoke. "I can't believe this!" Mirth spilled from his lips. "I cannot believe this."

"Me neither."

"What are the chances? Oh, wow. Oh, Miri..." He couldn't stop the tears from surfacing in his eyes. If this wasn't a miracle, he didn't know what was. Out of all the names they could have chosen...

She reached under the table and took his hand, their fingers interlacing.

This had to be one of the best days of his life.

She gestured to the screen with her chin. "Do you think that's why they moved? Because he died?"

He shrugged. "Could be. I think Sarah James might be a little more difficult to locate, though. Probably more Sarahs than Miltons." He frowned.

"*Jah*."

He gestured to the screen. "It looks like there are some Sarah Jameses on Facebook."

"I guess it's worth a shot."

"*Jah*, you can look at the photos to see if any of them look familiar." He clicked on the social media website, typed "Sarah James" into the search engine, and scrolled down the list of profiles. "Do any of these people look familiar?"

"*Nee*." She studied each profile picture carefully. "Wait. That one. Right there. That's her." She pointed excitedly to the screen.

He clicked on the profile, and his eyes roamed each photo.

The second he saw the picture, he knew it was his young son staring back at him. He had no doubt. He opened his mouth to speak, but emotion clogged his throat.

"That's our son." She squeezed his hand. "He looks just like you."

He nodded in silence, unable to tear his gaze away from the screen. "And you, too. *Ach*, he's the most beautiful child I've ever seen."

Miriam's chin quivered and she nodded.

"I'm going to make a printout of this. I don't know how well it will turn out, though." He closed his eyes. "*Denki, Gott.*"

Miri sighed deeply and closed her eyes.

"We don't have an address yet, though. And we can't access her personal details unless we're friends on Facebook."

She eyed him carefully. "Do you have a Facebook thing?"

"You mean, an account? No. And even if I did, the chances of her accepting a friend request from a complete stranger, and a man at that, is pretty much nil." He studied the profile, but his eyes kept straying back to the photo of their son. He could hardly peel his gaze away. But he needed to. They had to find this woman, to see if they could communicate with her somehow. "It doesn't look like she's posted anything lately, unless we can't see that info. It might only be available to her friends."

"At least we know she probably still lives in Indiana. Maybe we can search her name along with Indiana."

"Good idea." He opened up a different tab, not quite ready to close the Facebook page. "Just a sec. I'm going to talk to somebody about printing out that picture. You wanna scroll down and see if you can find something?"

"Sure."

Michael glanced back at Miri as he walked to the library help desk. "Could you help us print something, please? Neither one of us are all that experienced with the computer." He asked the female attendant.

"Sure." She rounded the desk and followed him back to where Miri sat.

Miri looked up. "Do you need me to move?"

"No, that's okay." The woman glanced at Michael. "What did you want to print?"

He reached down and clicked on the web page. "This photo."

"Sure. Did you save it yet?"

"No, how do I do that?"

"Just right click, then Save Picture As. You can just

save it to the desktop. It will erase off there when you log off." She showed them how to do what she'd just explained. "Then, just right click on the photo on the desktop, and click on Print. You want color, correct?"

Michael nodded. "Can we get two copies?" He winked at Miri and the corner of her lips curled up.

"Sure."

"Great." Michael smiled.

"Thank you," Miri said to the woman.

"It's printing now. You can pay at the front desk. It's fifteen cents for each color copy." She studied Michael. "Do you need anything else?"

"No, that's it. Thank you." He glanced toward the printer. "I can get them now?"

"Yes, they should be ready if you'd like to follow me to the front desk."

He fished thirty cents out of his pocket when she handed him the papers. "Thanks again."

A moment later, he was back at Miri's side. He grinned. "We have a picture of our son." He spoke the words quietly.

She nodded, but worry danced in her eyes. "Will you...keep mine at Sammy's for me?"

"Of course." But he knew it was only a matter of time before their community discovered they'd had a child together. He wouldn't kindle more angst for

Miri by mentioning it, though.

She gestured toward the screen. "I think I may have found an address. It's different than the one we have."

"Great. Let's write it down and see if we can find any others. Then we can send out a letter to see if it's her."

"*Jah.*"

"This is taking longer than I'd hoped."

She studied him. "Did you have other plans today?"

"No, not today. I mean, finding this lady."

"Well, at least we have a picture now."

"Yes, I'm very happy about that. I can't wait to show *Dawdi.*"

She shook her head. "I don't see any other addresses. Just this one."

"That must be it, then. Let's go?"

"*Jah.*"

His gaze traveled her face. "Would you...like to stop and grab and milkshake or a bite to eat? My treat."

She nodded, although he sensed timidity in the gesture.

If she considered this a date, and she'd just agreed to it, he would be over the moon. But he refused to assume anything. At this point in time, they were just friends. He'd have to be content with that. For now.

TWENTY-ONE

Miriam glanced over at Michael as he held the buggy reins in his hand. Something between them had shifted. And she liked it. Not that she fully trusted him now. But they were making forward progress. She'd only seen glimpses of this side of Michael when they'd dated several years ago. It was the part she'd fallen in love with.

But now? *Ach*, he seemed like a totally different person. Kind. Considerate. Even a little emotional. She hardly recognized him from the Michael who'd shown up in their community three months ago.

"Thanks for coming with me today." His eyes briefly met hers.

It hadn't lasted long enough for her liking. "I...I had a *gut* time."

"I'm glad." He looked as if he smiled to himself, like he harbored a secret only he was privy to.

"Do you think the post office will send out our letters today?" She clasped her hands in her lap.

"Might not be until Monday. But they were still open, so you never know."

"*Denki*, Michael."

His forehead creased. "For what?"

"For taking me along. For agreeing to go to the post office today. For buying me lunch."

"It was my pleasure. I loved every minute of it. I kind of hate to drop you off already."

Was he asking her to ride with him longer? Anticipation tickled her stomach. "We...we don't have to yet."

"You're sure? You want to ride longer?" He flicked an uncertain glance her way.

She nodded once.

His smile broadened and he turned off on the next country road. He gestured beyond them with his head. "Wanna go down to the creek?"

"Sure."

He pulled onto a smaller unpaved dirt road. "I sometimes go fishing here. Have you ever been?"

"I don't think so."

"It's a nice spot." He maneuvered the horse under a tree, then hopped down to secure the reins to a low-hanging branch.

She heard rushing water prior to stepping down from the buggy.

He held out his hand for her to grasp. "It's a little rugged."

She assented by taking his hand and followed him down the trail. "Do you come here often?"

"Only been twice since I've been back. The first time, with *Dawdi*, wasn't so *gut* because my casts were still on."

She carefully moved down the rocky embankment. Her eyes widened. "You walked down *this*? With a cast?"

"With *Dawdi's* help." He chuckled. "I was bored out of my mind and wanted something exciting to do. I'd been cooped up in that house too long. I think I was driving *Dawdi* crazy. He finally found an adventure for me."

"I can't imagine. But you always were a risk-taker."

He shrugged. "Not as much anymore."

Her brow shot up, but she said nothing.

Once they'd come to the bottom, Michael tugged on her hand, bringing her around to his side. He gestured to the scenery before them. "What do you think?"

She looked out at the stream, which flowed rapidly. "*Ach*! I never even knew this was here."

He crouched near the embankment, watching the water, then sat down on a boulder. "*Dawdi* said it all but dries up when it hasn't rained in a while. This is the most I've seen it running. Probably from that storm last week."

"It's *schee*." She glanced down at him and he patted the rock beside him.

"I can scoot over. I think we can both sit here."

She reluctantly lowered herself onto the rock.

They sat quietly for several moments, just listening to the sound of the water tumbling over the rocky creek bottom.

"This is so relaxing." She almost felt like removing her shoes and dipping her toes into the water.

"It is, isn't it? Nothing like sitting in a quiet place with nature all around you." He sighed. "I missed this when I was out in the *Englisch* world."

She swallowed, not wanting to entertain even a thought of the *Englisch* world.

"I'm done with that life." He shook his head. "I was so *dumm*."

"What makes you think you won't go back?"

"That is not what I desire anymore. I don't know how to explain it, but *Der Herr* has changed my heart. He's put new desires in there. Different ones."

"Like what?"

"Like joining the *g'may*. Like doing what *He* wants me to do." He shrugged and met her stare. "Maybe... having a family."

Her heartbeat quickened.

He stood, then moved to the edge of the creek. "I don't know. I look into that picture, into the eyes of our son. I just can't help but think that I've lost so much. Our boy missed out on knowing his real *daed* and *mamm*. And it's all my fault. We'll never get to know our son in his childhood years because of my immaturity, my foolishness. I've failed both you and him." When he turned to her, tears were shimmering in his eyes. "I'm so sorry, Miri." His voice cracked.

"*Ach*, Michael." She shot up and took a step toward him, her arms aching to comfort him. Moisture pricked her own eyes at the sight of this broken man before her. She opened her arms and drew him into them. "*Kumm*."

His body trembling, a hard sob expelled from his lungs. He grasped a hold of the back of her dress, pulling her tight against his heaving chest, clinging to her like a lifeline. "I'm sorry."

"I forgive you, Michael. I hope you can do the same for me."

He stepped back to survey her eyes, then nodded. "I accept full responsibility for what happened. You did nothing wrong. If I'd been there for you, you never would have given him up for adoption. Period. So, I don't want you feeling guilty."

She shook her head. "But I do. I could have kept him, raised him by myself. But I was too ashamed."

"Miri..." He sighed heavily, then lowered his head and sat down again.

"What?"

"No...I can't. At least, not now."

She touched his shoulder, demanding his attention. "I want to know what you were going to say." She planted herself on the boulder next to him.

He reached for her hand and held it between both of his, gently rubbing circles on her palm with his thumb. Something vulnerable wavered in his eyes. "I...I want to marry you."

Her heart clenched. She swallowed. "You do?" Her voice emerged as a breathless whisper.

He nodded once, his gaze lowering to her lips.

She leaned forward slightly, her heart racing, her eyes shutting. And she knew at that moment Michael Eicher was going to kiss her. And that she would willingly let him. And kiss him back.

His lips met hers in a gentle touch, tenderly caressing, exploring, causing her heartrate to spike beyond measure, it seemed. As she tilted her head, he deepened the kiss, his hands on her neck, fingers stroking her jawline, slipping under her *kapp*.

"Miri," he whispered. "I love you, Miri."

Then the spell was broken and he forced himself away. "I'm...I'm sorry...I shouldn't have done that."

"Why not?"

"I didn't ask you first."

"Yes, you did. You asked with your eyes, your body language."

"Still."

She reached her hand to his cheek, feeling the prickles of his five o'clock shadow. "I wanted you to."

His eyes studied her face, his look uncertain. "You did?"

"*Jah.*" She dipped her head, timid about her boldness.

"*Gut.*" He smiled and leaned forward, feathering her cheek with a kiss. "But if we're going to do this right, I can't give in to moments like that. We can't. Understand?"

Jah, she understood alright. And she knew it too. Kissing Michael Eicher was dangerous.

He stood from the boulder and offered his hand to her. "Let's get you home now."

She nodded and allowed him to help her up. But instead of letting go, he pulled her to his chest, took her face in his hands, and dropped his lips to hers once again. Warmth seemed to permeate every nerve ending in her body. Her arm meandered around his waist, her palm planted on his firm chest, his muscles tensing even more under her touch. This time, he held nothing back. His mouth tantalized hers with every blissful movement, his stubble burning her chin, until his lips left hers and traveled her jawline, her earlobe, her neck, her collar bone. *Ach.*

He groaned, then forced himself away from her. His breath hard and heavy. "Miri..." he breathed out. "I can't... Don't let me do that!"

Michael mentally chastised himself the entire way home. How could he allow himself to kiss Miri like that? *Ach*, he'd nearly...

He shook his head, refusing to ponder on it. He knew one thing and one thing for sure. *Nee*, make that two things.

One, when he was with Miriam Yoder, they kindled a wildfire that couldn't be contained. Two, he needed to marry her as soon as possible.

TWENTY-TWO

Michael bounced on his toes as he watched the road Miri would be walking down at any moment. A letter had been delivered today, addressed to the two of them. It had burned in his palm since the moment it arrived. He would have gone to fetch Miri himself, but she'd had errands to run this morning, so she'd been out of the house.

The second Miri walked through the door, he grasped her wrists and guided her to the table. "It's here. It came." He pushed the envelope toward her.

She sat down in one of the chairs; he did likewise. "You haven't opened it?"

He shook his head. "Not without you here."

She glanced around the room. "Is Sammy here?"

"*Nee*, he's visiting someone. It's just us." He probably would have taken her into his arms immediately if the matter before them wasn't so pressing. He *needed* to know what was in that letter.

He nudged the letter opener in her direction. "Go ahead."

Miri took the opener and slid it under the envelope's flap, then pulled out a folded single sheet of lined paper. She opened the paper and they both began reading silently.

Miriam and Michael,

I regret to inform you that your boy is no longer under my care. My husband recently passed away and, due to my own poor health, I am no longer able to care for him. This was not what I wanted but it was in his best interest. I wish I could have kept him, but my disease is terminal. I knew I had to make arrangements for my sweet boy sooner rather than later.

Since you didn't contact me after the adoption, I assumed you were still of the same mind. I was relieved when your letter came today. Last month I relinquished young Michael to the county foster care system, hoping he could find a forever home. I have included the name and phone number of the social worker I have been consulting, if you're inclined to contact her.

I hope all goes well with you.

Sincerely,
Sarah James

Michael's mouth dropped open and Miri turned her gaze on him. He had no words. He attempted to process what he'd just read. He reread the letter to make sure he'd understood the circumstances correctly.

Miri swallowed and finally found her voice. "So, he is living with strangers now?" Her brow furrowed.

"It would seem so." He reached for her hand. "Miri, are you thinking what I'm thinking?"

Her eyes flicked to the letter again. "I don't know."

"I think we need to contact this person. I'm not sure what the laws are, but...do you think it might be possible to get our son back? Would...would you want to?"

"*Ach*..." She shook her head. "I just...I thought...but he was adopted, he was safe." Tears surfaced in her eyes. "I wanted him to be with Sarah and Milton, not passed off to strangers."

"Maybe God has other plans for him. Think about it, Miri. We could get married and bring Michael to live with us...maybe. I feel like *Der Herr* is giving us a second chance. At love. At raising our son. At having a family. I don't want to let that chance slip through our fingers. And I don't think you want it to either. Am I right?"

Her chest heaved. "I...I don't know if I can do that, Michael." She swiped at her tears.

"Why?"

"I don't know if I trust you enough to be married...yet."

Michael's heart plunged. He reached for her hand. "*Ach*, Miri...I don't know what more I can do. I've tried to prove to you that I'm different now. Can't you see that?" He lifted her chin so she'd meet his eyes. "I've changed. I love you. I want to be with you forever."

She turned away, then stood from the table. She heaved a bitter sigh. "I need time. Time to pray."

"That's a good idea. Please pray about it. I'll do the same."

Except, their son may not have time. Who knew how long it might be before someone else wanted to adopt him? And if someone else did decide to adopt him, their chances of reclaiming their son would be impossible. Whether Miri agreed or not, he determined to contact the social worker. Today. He would take their son, even if he had to care for him by himself. If they'd let him.

"I don't know what to do, Sammy. I *want to* fully trust Michael. But I feel like agreeing to this might be foolish on my part. Disastrous, even. There's so much risk. What if I agree and he just disappears one day, leaving me and our child?"

Sammy's fingers steepled under his chin. "I suppose that *could* happen. But what if he *is* telling the truth? What if he *does* stay? What if he learns to become a *gut* father and a faithful husband? It seems to me like you could be making a mistake if you say no."

"I'm scared." Her chin quavered.

"There are no guarantees in life, that is for sure and certain. But I do know this. We cannot allow fear to make our decisions for us. We cannot allow fear to rule our lives. Many things we fear in life never come to fruition. Remember, *Gott* has not given us a spirit of fear."

"Do you think I should say yes, then?"

"That is a question only you can answer. You will have to live with whatever decision you make. I think you should pray and listen to the voice of *Gott*."

"I've been praying."

"What is He telling you to do?"

"I wish I knew for sure, but I don't. I mean, I *want* to be a mother to our child. And being happily married to your *gross sohn* sounds like a dream. But

I'm afraid that's *all* it is. I don't want to jump into a nightmare I cannot get out of. Do you understand?"

"I understand that you want to play it safe. Because if nothing changes, you won't lose anything. You won't get hurt, right?"

Safe. *Jah*, that was about the sum of it. She'd ventured beyond the safe zone once before. It had been a mistake that cost her dearly. Not only that, but it had been with Michael. And now, here he was again. Sweet talking her. Coaxing her. Tempting her. She'd given in last time and it proved to be a disaster. Who was to say this wouldn't end the same way?

What was the saying? *Fool me once, shame on you. Fool me twice, shame on me.* She'd already endured enough shame to last a lifetime.

"Sammy..." She couldn't hold in the sob escaping her lips. Her heart clenched. "I can't do this again."

Michael had a difficult time controlling his anger right about now. He crumpled up the note Miri had written him and tossed it against the wall. He fought the volley of curse words that threatened to escape his lips.

"No! This isn't supposed to happen, God!" He shouted.

Jah, he was upset with Miri. But he was even more upset with himself. *He* was the reason she could no longer trust. He never should have kissed her like he had. He'd probably frightened her away, made her remember his past behavior. Not only that, he'd given himself false hope.

He looked up to find his *grossdawdi* walking through the door. He hadn't even heard him approaching.

"*Ach, Dawdi.*"

He moved toward the kitchen table. "Trust *Der Herr's* timing, Michael. He knows what is best."

"But our son doesn't have time, *Dawdi.*" He frowned.

"Did you call the social worker?"

"I did. She advised me to hire a lawyer." He sighed and moisture burned in his eyes. "*Dawdi,*" his voice cracked, "I've made such a mess of my life."

Dawdi now stood in front of him and placed a hand on his shoulder. "*Gott* can fix the messes you've made. Do you believe that?"

"I do."

"Give Him your cares, *sohn*. Hand Him your broken pieces and He will mend them back together." He reached for his Bible in the center of the table. He flipped through the pages, then handed the open text to Michael. "Read what I have underlined."

Michael blinked away his tears, so he could see the words before him. "Behold, I make all things new."

"Allow *Der Her* to do what He does best. He is the Redeemer. He is the Healer. He is the Restorer. He can do these things in your life, but only if you permit Him to do so."

"But what about Miri?"

"Give her to Him too."

He swallowed. "Okay, *Dawdi*. Show me how."

Dawdi picked up his Bible. "Cast your cares upon Him, then rest on His promises, *sohn*. It's as simple and as difficult as that."

TWENTY-THREE

"**C**ongratulations, Michael. You've got the job."
Jason Byler shot his hand forward.

Michael shook his new boss's hand and sighed in relief. "Thank you. I really appreciate this."

"It's really fast-paced, so it may take you a while to get acclimated. Just take it in stride," his boss suggested, a friendly smile twinkling in his eyes.

Michael hoped the church didn't have any qualms about him working for an ex-Amish man. He probably should have discussed it with *Dawdi* prior to agreeing, but he'd needed a job badly. Not only would it provide much-needed income for lawyer and court fees, but it would keep his mind preoccupied so he wasn't dwelling on Miri and their son every other second of the day.

Miri had stopped coming to *Dawdi's* house altogether. He'd only seen her at church meeting, but she never looked his way. He'd been praying desperately for *Der Herr* to take the broken pieces of her heart and mend it back together. But a shattered heart took time and patience to heal, he'd realized. So he would allow God to do a work only He could do.

Meanwhile, he'd contacted a lawyer and she'd explained what his options were. First and foremost, he should petition the court for custody of his son. If his son was in foster care and eligible for adoption, he could apply to adopt their son.

He thought on his conversation with the lawyer.

"I'll be frank with you. This isn't typically a quick or easy process," the lawyer advised.

"What is involved?"

"If you're allowed to adopt, a home study will need to be conducted."

"What's a home study?"

"That is where the state assesses the dynamics of a family. They get to know you on a personal level. It's basically an in-depth investigation. If you have any skeletons in your closet, they will find them. It generally takes about six to eight weeks to complete the study. And you'll be required to have all the usual tests."

"Tests?"

"Fingerprints, medical examination, background

check, those sorts of things."

"And I'm guessing it's going to cost a lot of money, right?" He blew out a breath. At least he had a good job now.

"The total adoption process, not including the tests mentioned above, will be about three thousand dollars."

He swallowed. "Three thousand dollars?" He hadn't even begun making payments to the hospital yet.

"Yes."

"Just be thankful Indiana doesn't require foster parenting for children eligible for adoption. Because that would require many more months of training and at least six months of having your son in your home prior to adoption."

"Yes, I'm thankful for that."

He blew out a breath. This was a lot to take in. But getting their son back would be so worth it. He really wished Miri was onboard with this. It would make it much easier, and more enjoyable, if he had a companion in all of this.

He knew one thing. He needed to at least sit down with her and lay out all the facts. Perhaps, if she understood what he was willing to go through to get their son back, she'd learn to trust him again. He was determined to do whatever it took to open her eyes. But if they never opened, at least—hopefully—he'd have their son back. And right now, that was more than he could hope for.

TWENTY-FOUR

"What happened to your beau?" Miriam's brother Benny slapped a pair of mud-caked hands on the counter she'd just cleaned for the third time today.

She refrained from chastising the boy. "I don't have a beau," she said through gritted teeth.

"Uh huh, Michael Eicher. Everyone knows it."

Her heart sank. *Everyone?* "Did...did you talk to people about us?"

He nodded. "At school. Curly Dan said his sister saw you at the library and you were holding hands. And Eddie Stoltzfus saw you at Dairy Queen when he drove by with his *Daed's* driver. They know you and Michael have been kissing lots at Sammy's house."

She gasped. "We have *not* been kissing lots at Sammy's! Those are rumors and you and your classmates shouldn't be talking about other people.

It's called gossip. It's not what *Der Herr* wants us to do."

"Come on, Miri. Everyone knows you and Michael are getting hitched."

Miri? No one called her that except for Michael. "*Nee*, we are *not* getting hitched!" She turned on her heel and ran from the kitchen.

A moment later, she heard a knock on her bedroom door. She knew it was her *mamm* by the gentle rap on the wood frame. She quickly sat up and wiped her tears with her dress sleeve. "*Kumm* in."

The door opened and her mother walked in, closing it behind her. "I overheard your conversation with Benny." *Mamm* frowned and moved to sit on the edge of her bed.

"I wish people would just mind their own business."

The edge of *Mamm's* mouth turned up slightly. "You and Michael are the most exciting thing that's happened since Ella and Melvin's wedding last year. Keeping quiet would be like asking a nightingale not to sing."

Miriam groaned. "There is no me and Michael."

Mamm traced the quilt pattern with her index finger. She and *Mamm* had begun piecing it together on her fifteenth birthday. They'd taken an entire year to do it, working on it little by little. On her sixteenth birthday, it had gone into her dower chest, intending to stay there until she married. But when she returned from the *Englisch* world, all hopes of finding someone to marry had been dashed into pieces. So she'd begun using the quilt. No sense in having it go to waste.

Mamm's hand covered hers. "I know you don't want to talk about it, but it's time, Miriam."

She swallowed. "Talk about what?"

"About what happened when you left the *g'may* for a time. You went to be with Michael Eicher, ain't so?" *Mamm's* brow raised slightly.

Miriam gasped. "Is that how the rumor mill was turning?"

"It is true, *ain't not*?"

"The truth is that I didn't leave to seek out Michael. Nor did I see him while I was living in the *Englisch* world."

"Then why did you leave?"

Tears came full force now and she couldn't stop them. Her chest heaved with anguish. Guilt and shame had become such a dominant part of her life. It would feel *gut* to be able to release it, to finally reveal her secrets. She was *so* tired of living a lie.

"I left to...to have his *boppli*!" She blurted the words out. She couldn't meet her mother's gaze, but she didn't miss the huff of air expelling from her lips.

"Miriam..." *Mamm* moved close and gathered her into her arms. "*Ach*, Miriam. I had no idea you were in the *familye* way."

"I didn't know what kind of *bu* Michael was. I just thought he was a flirt. But when Michael asked me home from a singing, I didn't know we'd end up courting. I didn't expect to fall in love with him. I didn't expect him to leave. I didn't expect to be in the *familye* way." She blew her nose on tissue. "*Mamm*, I was so scared."

Mamm rubbed her back. "I know."

"I prayed. I prayed so hard because I didn't know what to do. Then I saw one of those signs along the road. You know the one that asks if you are pregnant and scared? And that was *me*. So I called the number and the people helped me. They helped me leave. They helped me find a place to stay. They took care of me. And they helped me find someone to take the *boppli*. To adopt him."

"*Ach*, Miriam."

She knew *Mamm* was disappointed. She could hear it in her tone. That was one thing she'd learned to do well. Disappoint people. Was there *anything* in this life she'd gotten right? She didn't think so.

"I thought I would feel better after I gave the baby

up, like my problems would just miraculously go away. But I could never forget my sweet boy." Wetness seemed to be a permanent part of her face lately. She didn't bother to wipe her tears, and the salty drops rolled to her lips. "*Mamm*, it was so hard."

"Did Michael even know? Did you tell him?"

She shook her head. "Not then, but he does now."

"And?"

"He wants to marry me. He wants to try to get our *boppli* back."

"I don't think that's possible, is it? Not with adoption."

"*Nee*, it isn't. But his adoptive *daed* died and his adoptive *mamm* is real sick. He's in foster care now."

"And Michael *wants* the *boppli*?"

"*Jah*."

"Miriam, this sounds like something you might want to consider. If Michael is offering to marry you and you can get the *boppli* back—"

"Don't you see? I'm not worthy to be his *mamm*! I gave him away." She realized then that it was *herself* she didn't trust, not Michael. He had proven himself. When Sammy sequestered her after church, she'd learned that Michael had even hired a lawyer to help try to get their *boppli* back. He'd also gotten a woodworking job nearby. That didn't sound like a man intent on leaving the community.

"There isn't one person in this world *worthy* of that honor, *dochder*. But it seems to me that *Der Herr* gave Michael's child to *you* for a reason. He doesn't make mistakes. It sounds like He's giving you both, *nee, all three of you* a second chance."

And in that moment, she broke completely.

TWENTY-FIVE

Michael hadn't expected to see Miri sitting on *Dawdi's* porch swing the minute he'd guided Dr. Seuss into the yard. He looked down at his filthy clothes and grunted. Too bad she hadn't arrived after he showered, when he'd look and feel good. But just the sight of her was a blessing, so he'd take what he could get.

Dawdi met him as he stepped from the buggy, offering to take care of Dr. Seuss. "You have more pressing matters." He flicked a glance toward Miri.

Michael lowered his voice. "Why is she here?"

"She wants to talk to you."

Anticipation swirled in his chest. Would this be a positive visit or a negative one? He never knew with Miri. Just when he thought he'd been making progress with her, she shied away. But if Michael was anything, he was persistent.

He strode across the yard then approached the house, slowing his gait. He stepped onto the porch, sucking in a fortifying breath. "Hello, Miri."

"Will you sit here?" She touched the porch swing seat next to her.

Being that close to her probably wouldn't be a wise move on his part. He shook his head and leaned back against the railing a couple feet away. Better to be safe than sorry. He crossed his arms over his chest. "I'll just stand here."

She nodded and her eyes lowered to the floor boards on the porch.

"You wanted to say something?" He refrained from tapping his foot. He wished she'd just get on with it, especially if it was something bad.

"I..." She swallowed. "I told my *mamm*. About us. About the *boppli*."

"You did? What did she say?"

She lifted her head now and stared into his eyes. "She thinks that *Der Herr* is giving us another chance. To raise our son. To have a family."

"And what do *you* think?" His heartbeat doubled. *God, please.*

"I think she might be right."

"What are you saying? Does this mean you'll give us—give *me*—a chance?"

A beautiful smile slowly crossed her lips. "It does."

Had he heard her right? "You...are you serious?"

"I am."

He took two steps forward, but instead of sitting down, he stood in front of her, leaning forward and placing each of his hands on the porch swing behind her near her shoulders. He bent down and dropped his head to meet her lips with his. "*Denki*, Miri." He pulled back and chuckled. "I hope you're not offended by my sweaty body."

Her brow shot up and a smirk surfaced. "I mostly smell sweet sawdust. And I like it. I think I can get used to you returning home from work every day smelling like this."

Home from work? Every day? He swallowed. "You could?"

She slid her hand up his chest and grasped one of his suspenders, then yanked him close again. "I definitely could." To his delight, *she* kissed *him* this time.

He leaned close and whispered in her ear, "I love it when you get aggressive."

A throat cleared loudly behind them as *Dawdi* stepped onto the porch. Michael moved back, then took a seat beside her on the swing.

Dawdi chuckled. "By the look of it, I'm guessing she changed her mind."

Michael reached for her hand and intertwined their fingers. "Yes, she did."

"*Gut.*" *Dawdi* nodded. "What's the next step?"

"We still need to talk about that." Michael glanced at Miri.

"I'll leave you two to *talk* then." *Dawdi* chuckled then stepped into the house.

Michael waited for the door to close before pulling Miri onto his lap. "Where were we?"

A tap on the front window forced them apart. *Dawdi* pulled back the curtain and shook his head. "That doesn't look like talking to me," his muffled voice came through the glass.

Miri giggled. "I think we'd better just talk." Her hand caressed his jaw and she lifted a brow. "For now."

He cleared his throat as she slid off his lap. "*Jah,* that sounds *gut* to me. We'll talk now."

"Unless if you need a shower, I can make supper."

"You're staying a while, then?"

"I'd planned to. You know, to talk."

"*Jah,* to talk." He winked.

Miriam rinsed the supper dishes and prepared the water for washing. A smile teased her lips as she thought of a future with Michael. They really did make a *gut* couple.

"*Denki* for saving me from fixing supper tonight. Michael and I have been taking turns, so I'm glad you came over on my night." Sammy handed her his plate and winked. "I never realized how spoiled we'd become until you stopped coming around. But you two have things to discuss now. Let me wash up these dishes." He scooted her out of the way.

"You're sure?" Miriam frowned. "It won't take me long."

"*Jah*, I'm sure. You two *chust* need to stay in view." His head leaned to the left. "You can sit at the table there so I can add my two cents to the conversation."

"And I thought it was to keep me in line." Michael's eyes sparkled with mischief, as they reflected the color of his shirt. Man, he sure cleaned up nicely.

"That too." Sammy thrust a wooden spoon in his direction.

"Is that a threat, *Dawdi*?" Michael chuckled.

"It's whatever it needs to be."

Miriam enjoyed their banter.

"And before you get any other notions," Sammy looked to both of them, wooden spoon still firmly pointed in their direction, "I want you two to live *here* after you're hitched."

Michael sighed heavily. "But then I can't chase her around the house n—"

Miriam gasped at his boldness, and playfully slapped him on the arm.

"You're two seconds away from this spoon, boy," Sammy threatened, a tease in his tone. "And I don't think there will be any 'chasing around' with a small *bu* and your *grossdawdi* here, now, will there?"

"With strategic planning..." Michael shrugged and winked at Miriam.

She shook her head. "*Ach...*"

"You're making her blush now." Sammy's sympathetic tone endeared him to her even more.

"Sammy, it would be an honor to live here." Miriam approached Sammy, patted him on the back, and smiled.

He sighed and tears shimmered in his eyes. "It will be nice to have a female in this house again."

Michael lifted his cup of coffee in the air and raised his eyebrows twice. "I second that." His eyes roamed Miriam's dress.

"That's it. You're grounded, *bu*." Sammy shook his head, then turned to Miriam. "You'll have to forgive my *gross sohn*. He's been in the *Englisch* world far too long. He's forgotten what it means to be a *gut* Amish *bu*." He pointed to Michael. "And you. You are going to memorize a chapter of the Bible tonight."

Michael grinned. "The Song of Solomon?"

"*Nee*. Leviticus."

Miriam couldn't help but laugh at the look of horror on Michael's face.

Sammy leaned over. "And he thinks I'm joking. I'm not."

Miriam laughed again. "Well then, it looks like I'd better leave early tonight."

Michael shook his head. "You're not going anywhere, future *fraa*." He grasped her hand and led her back to the table.

"About your plans...you need to talk to the leaders," Sammy suggested, all joking aside. "You will probably need to make a confession."

Miriam's head lowered. "That's the part I've been dreading."

"A confession before the *g'may* will help silence gossip," Sammy said.

"Or fuel it," Michael said wryly.

"Everyone sins. The people understand that." Sammy looked at both of them. "It will clear the air. And when you bring your *bu* home, nobody will ask you about it because they'll already know."

"You have a point." Michael nodded. "But I'm not a member yet."

"They have agreed to accept your membership from Pennsylvania."

Michael's brow shot up. "Really?"

Sammy nodded. "They've been watching you."

"They have?" Michael looked to Miriam. Hopefully no one had spied on them when they were down at the creek. Because if they had, she was certain his membership would not be approved. And they both might be required to make a confession.

"Apparently, they approve of what they've seen."

"That's *gut* news. I'll have to watch my step then." Michael blew out a breath. "Will they want us to marry right away?" His gaze flicked to hers.

"I would imagine so. You've already..." Sammy's voice trailed off.

"*Jah.*" Miriam nodded.

"And what about the *bu*?" Sammy stared at Michael.

"I've filed the papers. My lawyer said it might be months before it goes to court. In the meantime, we wait." Michael reached over and squeezed her hand. "And pray."

TWENTY-SIX

Miriam attempted to keep her hands from shaking as she prepared snacks for the guests who would be visiting that evening.

An arm slipped around her waist. Michael leaned close and whispered in her ear, "You ready for this?"

"*Nee*. I'm nervous."

He turned her to look at him, then reached up and caressed her cheek with the back of his fingers. "There's nothing to be nervous about, *Schatzi*."

"Michael." She sighed. "I got pregnant out-of-wedlock, left the community for two years, gave our baby up for adoption, then kept it all a secret. Until now."

"What can they do to you? To us?"

"I don't know, not let us get married?"

"Seriously? If anything, they'll make us get married sooner. I just don't see how that's a bad thing. We already know we won't be getting married during the wedding season, so who cares? We already know people are gossiping about us and will continue to do so, but who cares? People are going to do what they're going to do. All we need to do is follow *Der Herr* and trust Him to direct our paths, ain't so?" He lifted her chin, then briefly brushed her lips with his. "We're in this together and *Gott* is with us."

She nodded. *Ach*, how much Michael had grown in his faith! She never would have dreamed it. Although, he still possessed a mischievous streak—which she secretly enjoyed.

The moment they heard commotion outside the door, Michael stepped away. This meeting would consist of Miriam, her folks, Michael, Sammy, the deacon, two ministers, and the bishop. Miriam now wondered what the leaders expected to hear at this meeting Sammy had called them to. Were they just expecting an engagement announcement, or were they privy to any of the details that were to be discussed?

Sammy ushered in *Mamm* and *Daed*, followed by the leaders.

Michael looked at her and winked. "Looks like it's showtime."

She shook her head. How could he joke at a time like this?

Mamm joined her in the kitchen, while Michael slipped out to join the men. *Mamm* came close and helped her finish putting a slice of zucchini bread on each guest's plate. The water for the coffee was hot and she had iced tea at the ready as well.

Fortunately, her folks liked Michael Eicher and were very much in favor of their union. Of course, Michael was the type of guy who pretty much got along with or could charm anybody. She was glad that her folks were already aware of the past, so when they confessed it would not come as a surprise to them.

As soon as their guests were served, they'd bowed for the silent prayer, and everyone was seated around the table, Sammy took the initiative to speak first. "Michael and Miriam have a couple of issues to discuss with you today." He gestured for Michael to take the helm.

Michael cleared his throat. "When Miriam and I dated five years ago, we...uh...shared the marriage bed, resulting in a baby being conceived. The baby was put up for adoption when it was born, but due to unfortunate events, our son is now in foster care. We're now trying to get custody of our son again, but we're waiting on a court date."

The bishop nodded for Michael to continue.

"And...Miriam and I would like to get married."

The bishop looked to the other leaders to gauge their responses. "I'm guessing your families are in agreement?" He turned to *Mamm* and *Daed*.

"We are," *Daed* said the words, but Miriam noted the redness of his face and neck. Clearly, he was ashamed of Miriam and Michael's actions, although he'd never said as much.

"Normally, we would have you make a confession before the church and put you both in the *ban* for six weeks. However, since your situation is unique, I think a confession before the *g'may* will be sufficient. A *ban* would likely be difficult to uphold given the circumstances." He turned to the other leaders. "What are your thoughts?"

John Troyer, one of the ministers, spoke up, alarm in his tone. "You are not concerned this will encourage wantonness amongst our *youngie*?"

"I think a pregnancy out-of-wedlock with a child under the supervision of the government, combined with a wedding out-of-season is sufficient warning for our young folks." The deacon concurred with the bishop.

"You have a *gut* point." The other minister added his two cents. His eyes trained on the bishop. "When will they marry?"

The bishop frowned, rubbing his wiry white

beard. "Due to the manner in which Michael and Miriam have gone about this, I do not feel it is our place to sanction the marriage." He turned to Michael. "I think it would be best if your ceremony is conducted by a justice of the peace."

Mamm gasped the same time Miriam sucked in a breath. Not even an Amish wedding? She hung her head, begging her tears not to fall. She didn't dare look up at *Daed*.

The minister spoke up again, facing the other leaders. "How do you feel about enacting the *ban* once they are married? I feel strongly that something other than a confession is necessary."

"I have to agree with John," the other minister said. "A mere confession seems too light a consequence."

"Very well. We will vote during the next meeting." The bishop nodded to the other leaders. He turned to Michael, but glanced at Miriam as well. "You will be seeing the justice of the peace soon then, I presume?"

Michael studied Miriam, his mien hovering between remorseful and excited. She dipped her head slightly.

"*Jah*, we will take care of that," Michael stated.

More than anything, Miriam just wanted their company to be gone, so she could break down in Michael's arms.

Michael hung up the phone on the shanty wall. He turned to Miri, who sat waiting on the lone plastic chair. "Okay, they said we will need proof of residency, identity, and date of birth." Michael frowned. "And a Social Security number. And they need our folks' names and the state where they were born."

"What does all that mean? Proof of residency?"

"I'm not entirely sure. But I think..." He stared down at the list he'd written. "Do you have a driver's license?"

"From when I was *Englisch*. It's in my secret box."

"And a Social Security number?"

"*Jah*. They said I had to have it for a job."

"What about a birth certificate?"

She nodded. "I couldn't get my Social Security card without it, so I ordered one. I had to have all of those things for the adoption too."

"Okay. She said we could bring two pieces of mail each, showing our address for the residency part." He chuckled wryly. "My hospital bills should vouch for that."

"Do you know where your folks were born?"

He nodded. "Both in Pennsylvania. How about yours?"

"I think maybe Indiana and Michigan? I can ask."

He rubbed his hands together. "Well, it looks like we're set to get our marriage license then." He couldn't tamp down his excitement and drew her near. "In two days, I'll make you my *fraa*."

"*Jah*." Her chin quivered.

He slipped his fingers under it, raising her eyes to meet his. "I'm going to do everything in my power so you don't regret marrying me for even a minute, Miriam Yoder."

At her nod, he bent down and pressed his lips to hers. Making Miri his *fraa* would be a dream come true.

❧

"You're *what*?" Nora practically hollered the words. "Wait! It sounds like I've been missing out on a whole lot here. You *cannot* be getting married to Michael Eicher!"

Miriam suppressed a smile. "I am. Tomorrow. And I want you to be there."

"Okay, rewind." Nora held up a hand. "Tell me *right now*. Are you in the *familye* way?"

"*Nee*."

"Don't tell me you're leaving the *g'may*. You're not going to become *Englisch* with Michael."

"*Nee*, Michael's becoming Amish. Or, I should say, he's rejoining the church."

"I'm still not getting this. Help me out, Miriam. Why the courthouse?"

She sighed heavily. "I guess you'll find out soon enough anyhow."

"Find out *what*?"

"Michael and I already had a *boppli* together."

"*What*?" Nora bellowed.

"We have a little boy. His name is Michael. He's four years old."

"You better be making this up."

"I'm not. That's why I left to live in the *Englisch* world." She sucked in a breath. "We will make a confession at the next church meeting. And we will be under the *ban* for six weeks."

Nora's mouth hung open. "You're not joking."

Miriam shook her head. "Will you come? Stand with me? At my wedding?"

"Yes. Sure. Absolutely." Nora pulled Miriam in for a fierce hug. "Why didn't you tell me any of this until now?"

"I don't know. I was scared, I guess." She shrugged. "Then when Michael came back, so did our past. We couldn't ignore it."

"Where is your little boy?"

"He had been adopted, but he's in foster care now. Michael and I want to try to get him back."

"Oh, wow." Nora shook her head. "You think you know a guy."

"But you were right about Michael. He's different now. He's changed. Matured."

"Good. I'm glad to hear that. I'll be there tomorrow. Ten o'clock sharp. With a camera."

"A camera?" Miriam's jaw went slack.

"It's an *Englisch* wedding. Why not?" She winked. "I won't tell if you won't."

TWENTY-SEVEN

Miriam stood next to Michael, a man in a black robe stood in front of them holding a Bible in his hands.

"Do you have the rings?"

Michael looked at Miriam and frowned. "Uh...do we *need* to have rings? We do not wear rings in the Amish."

The justice of the peace eyed their attire and shrugged. "I guess it's not *required*. Do you exchange something else, then?"

"No. Just vows before God." Michael cast a half smile in her direction.

"Okay, then." He glanced down at a slip of paper in his open Bible. "We are gathered together today in the sight of God and these witnesses to join Michael Eicher and Miriam Yoder in holy matrimony."

Miriam glanced behind her at Nora, whose smile

could have lit up the entire room.

"Michael, do you take Miriam to be your lawfully wedded wife? For better or worse, for richer or poorer, in sickness and in health? To have and to hold, to love, honor, and cherish as long as you both shall live?" The justice of the peace waited for Michael's response.

Michael nodded and took ahold of her hand. "Yes. I do." He smiled confidently.

"And do you, Miriam, take Michael to be your lawfully wedded husband? For better or worse, for richer or poorer, in sickness and in health? To have and to hold, to love, honor, and cherish as long as you both shall live?"

She nodded and squeezed Michael's hands. "I do."

"I'm going to change this script a little bit, since you're not exchanging rings." The man said. "Michael, will you take both of Miriam's hands in yours?"

He did as asked.

"Michael, repeat after me. With this vow, I thee wed. And pledge my constant faith and abiding love."

Michael repeated the words, with tears shimmering in his eyes.

The justice of the peace continued. "Miriam, please repeat after me: With this vow, I thee wed. And pledge my constant faith and abiding love."

She repeated likewise, squeezing Michael's hands.

"By the authority vested in me by the state of Indiana, I now pronounce you husband and wife. Michael, you may kiss your bride."

Miriam's eyes widened when Michael leaned forward and gently brushed his lips with hers. In plain sight of several strangers, Nora, and Sammy! Thankfully, her folks hadn't come. *Ach*, the *Englisch* ways never ceased to astound her. Of all the things she imagined today, she'd never dreamed of the first kiss by her husband being in public.

Michael had insisted on treating his bride to a fancy meal after the ceremony. They opted to stay the night in a hotel instead of returning home right away. *Dawdi* had told him to take his time and to be sure to spoil her. And spoil her, he had in mind to do. Whatever she wanted.

Their taxi driver dropped them off in front of the hotel they'd be spending the night in. He loved watching Miri's expressions. First, when they'd pulled up to the expensive high-rise hotel. Then, when they'd walked into the hotel's fancy lobby. A stunning chandelier hung from the ceiling, its crystals projecting glorious rainbows of color on the walls. He was certain she'd never seen anything so extravagant.

They strolled up to the check-in desk, hand-in-hand. "We have a reservation for tonight. The name is Michael Eicher."

The receptionist typed his name into the computer in front of her, surveyed them carefully—a smile playing on her lips—then nodded. "The Honeymoon Suite?"

He glanced at Miri. "Yep, that's the one."

"I'll need to see your ID and credit card, please."

He dug into his pants pocket and fished them out of his wallet.

"Thank you." She handed him a receipt, along with two cards in an envelope. She pointed beyond them. "To the elevators. Then to the fifteenth floor. You'll see signs on the wall with room numbers."

"Okay, I think we'll find it. Thank you." He took Miri's hand in his again, pulling their lone suitcase along in the other. "I can't wait to see our room."

"Have you been here before?" Miri took everything in, which was fine with him—for now. Eventually, he'd want her focus solely on him.

"No, but I've read good things about it." He pushed the Up button on the elevator control panel.

"It's so fancy." The elevator dinged and the doors opened for them. Fortunately, the elevator was empty. They quickly stepped inside and he pushed in the number of the floor their room was located on.

"Nothing but the best for my bride." As soon as the doors closed, he pulled her into his arms and dropped his lips to hers. It was the first moment of privacy they'd had since the ceremony, and he'd been dying to kiss his new bride.

He pulled away when the elevator came to a halt at the fifth floor. The doors opened and three people stepped in. So much for privacy. The elevator made two more stops before finally arriving at their designated floor.

Miriam nearly swooned the moment she'd walked into their Honeymoon Suite. Her new husband had been nothing but surprises since they'd said "I do." She was sure no other Amish woman alive had been this spoiled on her wedding night.

Normally, after a full day of activities and feasting, an Amish couple would spend the night at the bride's folks' place. The next day, they'd have to clean up from the festivities the day before. She'd half-expected to feel depressed because she hadn't participated in an Amish wedding ceremony of her own. Should she feel guilty that she was actually happy with the way things turned out? No stress, no clean-up required, no lack of privacy. *Jah*, she kind of liked it this way. She'd certainly have a story to tell that was different from everyone else's.

Michael Eicher had so far proved to be a first-rate husband.

A chilled bottle of sparkling cider awaited them in their room, along with chocolate-covered strawberries, and a lovely bouquet of red roses. Her face had nearly caught fire when her husband pointed out the jacuzzi tub for two. The hotel had even provided robes for them to wear. One of her favorite features was their private balcony with a view overlooking the city. She could only imagine how gorgeous it would be when the sun completely disappeared, the darkness emerged, and the city lights took on an electric glow.

Michael mentioned that he'd also purchased tickets for a theatre production, but it wouldn't start for several hours. They had the entire afternoon to themselves for rest, relaxation, and romance.

Truly, this would be a night she'd never forget.

TWENTY-EIGHT

Neither Michael nor Miriam had expected the reception they'd received at *Dawdi's* when they returned home from their brief honeymoon. Several close friends and family members had greeted them with food and gifts and well wishes. *Dawdi* and Miri's friend Nora had planned the entire event.

Michael was happy their family celebrated the event, although the community as a whole had not.

Even so, they were glad for some peace and quiet when all their guests drove home for the evening.

Dawdi yawned then stood from his chair. He eyed Michael and Miri as they cuddled on the couch. "Guess it's time for me to turn in. Oh, and before I forget, some mail came for you today, Michael." He pointed to the desk in the corner. "Well, good night you two."

"Good night, *Dawdi*," they said in unison as he disappeared down the hall.

Michael turned to his wife of one day. "What about you, *fraa*?" He raised his eyebrows twice. "You ready to turn in too?" His fingers slowly slid down her arm.

"Are you?'

"Only if you are."

"I am a little tired after the commotion of the last couple of days, not that I mind." She leaned over and kissed him on the mouth. It was something he'd never tire of. She unfastened one of the buttons of his shirt, then two, teasing him. "Why don't I go get ready for bed while you read your mail?"

Ach, he didn't care a lick about his mail right now. He wanted to follow his *fraa*. "*Jah*, okay."

As she stepped into the bathroom, he closed his eyes, recalling the intimate moments they'd shared in their hotel room. Hot anticipation flowed through his entire body at the thought of his *fraa* sharing his bed tonight. He'd dreamed of this night since the day he'd arrived at *Dawdi's*. He could hardly believe he was married to Miriam Yoder. The woman of his dreams.

He'd better hurry up and read his blasted mail before his *fraa* fell asleep without him. He hurried to *Dawdi's* desk and stopped short when he noticed a handwritten envelope addressed to him. The handwriting appeared to be feminine in nature. The other piece of mail seemed official looking. Had they secured a court date?

He hastily tore open the envelope and read the words on the page. "Yes!" In just over a month, he'd be able to speak to a judge about reclaiming his and Miri's son. He couldn't wait to share the news with his *fraa*.

He quickly opened the second envelope. It was only a single page. One paragraph, in fact. One paragraph that had the potential to change the rest of his life. He carefully read the words over and over again, to be sure he hadn't missed the "just kidding" line. But there was no such line. Only the stark truth.

There was a very real possibility that he was HIV positive. And if that was the case, his brand-new wife was now too.

Miriam stepped into Sammy's darkened living room. She'd gone to the bedroom nearly thirty minutes ago, but Michael never joined her. Surely he'd finished reading his mail by now.

"Michael? Are you in here?"

Silence answered back.

Goosebumps suddenly prickled on her arms. Something wasn't right.

She heard a faint squeaking sound. The porch swing. What was Michael doing? He'd said he'd be in shortly. Perhaps he'd just needed some fresh air.

She sighed, then stepped out onto the porch. The breeze caused her to shiver in her thin nightgown. Or maybe the shiver was from something else entirely. "Michael? What are you doing out here?"

"Miri?" His voice cracked with emotion. Something was definitely wrong. "I...I couldn't come in."

She moved to sit next to him on the porch swing. She took his hand in hers. "What's wrong?"

"I don't know if I can tell you." Anguish poured from his lips. She'd never seen Michael in such a state.

"What do you mean?"

"I may have ruined our lives."

"What?"

"Miri," he released a hard sob, "I think I'm HIV positive."

"But we..."

"I'm sorry, Miri. I had no idea."

She shot up from the swing and shook her head. "This is not happening."

"I'm sorry."

"You're *sorry*?" Her eyes filled with moisture. "You've given me a *gift* that will effectively reduce my life by decades and...you're *sorry*? I knew this was too good to be true."

"Miri, I didn't know! If I did, I never would have married you."

"You didn't think to get tested *before* asking me to marry you?"

"Why would I? I'm perfectly healthy. And I...I took certain measures." He squeezed his eyes shut. "Did *you* get tested?"

The accusation in his voice flared her anger. How dare he turn this on her! "I've been with one person, Michael. One. My husband."

"Well, what do you want me to do about it?"

"I don't know. All I know is that marrying you was a mistake." She turned on her heel and stormed back into the house alone. What on earth had she done? She should have never agreed to marry Michael Eicher. Tears watered her pillow until she'd finally drifted off into a fitful sleep.

TWENTY-NINE

Michael awakened to a firm hand nudging his shoulder. He attempted opening his eyes, but his eyelashes seemed melded shut from the onslaught of grief he'd endured the night before. His heart still physically ached from Miri's rejection and the sorrow he'd caused her. What kind of a husband was he?

He sat up, swiping the fresh barrage of tears.

"*Ach*, Michael. What is going on? Why are you sleeping out here on the couch? Where is your *fraa*?" He couldn't even process all of *Dawdi's* words, his mind thick with emotions he'd never experienced.

"Miri...she's not here?" His voice trembled.

"*Nee*. No sign of her this morning." *Dawdi* frowned. "What's going on, Michael?"

"I blew it, *Dawdi*."

"What do you mean?"

Michael moved to the desk, where he'd left the letter last night. He handed it to *Dawdi*. "Read this."

Dawdi's eyes quickly scanned the words on the page. "You know this woman?"

He shrugged. "In a manner of speaking, I guess you can say that. Not well at all." In fact, he barely remembered her.

"And you told Miriam?"

"I did. Because she likely has HIV now too."

"Likely? But you are not sure? I think you should be tested, ain't so?"

"I plan to do that today." He placed a hand on his *grossdawdi's* shoulder. "*Dawdi*, will you pray for me? For us?"

Dawdi nodded. "*Jah*, I will pray for you right now." He bowed his head and Michael followed suit. When he'd finished, his head rose and he stared Michael in the eye. "Whatever the outcome, *Der Herr* will be with you, *sohn*. He will never leave you."

And in that moment, Michael drew *Dawdi* tight, and broke down once again.

Michael figured it would be best to give Miri time to process their new revelation. He hadn't even had the opportunity to share the good news with her yet, news of their court hearing. But...would the judge deny them custody of their son if they tested positive for HIV? The thought bothered him more than he cared to admit.

"*Ach, Gott.* I have done so many things wrong. Please untangle this mess I've made of my life. Please, at the very least, bring my *fraa* back to me."

His driver stopped in front of the pharmacy and Michael hopped out. "I shouldn't be long."

He jogged into the store, hoping he wouldn't see anyone he knew. He quickly found the test, grabbed a couple other things so as not to appear conspicuous or draw attention to the test box. Once it was paid for, he slipped the box into the beanie he'd just purchased. He wished they'd had flowers available. He could have purchased some for Miri. Not that it would make a difference.

How could he have gone from the best day of his life to the worst in less than twenty-four hours?

It was been mid-morning when Miriam stumbled back onto Sammy's property. She'd hoped a trip down to the creek would clear her head, but it hadn't. She'd been relieved when she spied Michael leaving with a driver. She couldn't face him this morning. Not after all that had been said between them last night.

She'd been fooling herself, entertaining a fairytale, believing that she and Michael Eicher could actually have a happy life together. But that was *all* it was—a fairytale.

She pulled the screen door open and stepped into Sammy's house like she had a thousand times before. Sammy sat at the table, Bible open in front of him, sipping a cup of coffee. He glanced up from his meditation, an empathetic smile gracing his lips.

"Is there more hot water?" She walked into the kitchen.

"*Jah*, on the stove."

She scooped a serving of instant coffee into a mug and added the simmering water.

"There are some eggs in the pan as well. I saved some for you."

"*Ach*, Sammy. I'm sorry. I should have been the one to make breakfast." She dished a little onto her plate, along with a slice of bread.

"You had other things on your mind this morning, ain't so?"

"*Jah*." She slid into her chair at the table, then bowed her head in silent prayer. Steam rising from her coffee mug cautioned her to think twice before indulging in a sip.

Sammy's wizened hand slid across the table and covered hers. "Want to talk about it, *maedel*?"

"I think I made a mistake." Her heart squeezed tight at the words.

"Marrying *mei gross sohn*?"

She nodded.

"Why did you marry him?"

She shrugged. "I thought it made sense. We have a *boppli* together. I thought he'd changed. He asked me to marry him. I loved him."

"But now?"

"Now, I just don't know. I don't know if it's enough."

"Do you still love him?"

"I think so."

"Did you expect your life to be perfect?"

"*Nee*, I did not. But I didn't expect *this*."

"When you marry someone, you marry every part of them. The good and the bad. Including their past mistakes."

Her lips curved downward. "I've never thought of it that way."

"You promised to love him for better or worse, in sickness and in health."

"I know."

"Do you know what love does?"

She shook her head.

"Love covers a multitude of sins. Jesus was our example of this. True love knows no bounds." Sammy's words pierced her heart.

He stood from the table, slid his closed Bible back to the center, and placed his empty coffee cup on the counter. "You and Michael need each other right now. Don't allow the enemy to tear you apart."

Miriam nodded and watched Sammy walk out the back door. She needed to spend some time in prayer.

The screen door groaned in protest as Michael hefted it open and stepped into the house. He hadn't seen anyone outside, so he guessed *Dawdi* must be inside. He wondered if Miri had returned. With all his heart, he hoped she hadn't gone back to her folks' place. He'd be devastated if he'd lost her for good.

The moment he saw her standing at the sink, his heart plunged into his gut. *Thank you for bringing her home, Gott.* He had no idea what words to say to her to fix their situation. He'd already apologized. Of course, he realized a mere apology could not erase their circumstances or smooth away the hurt he'd caused.

He refrained from approaching her, but instead

dropped his purchases off in their bedroom. *Their* bedroom. The one his brand-new *fraa* had slept in alone last night. *Way to go, Michael. Best Husband of the Year Award right there.* He squeezed his eyes shut against the self-deprecation threatening to overtake him.

Desperation clawed at him. He needed to make things right, but hadn't a clue how to accomplish that task. *God, I need Your help.*

With purposeful steps, he strode toward the kitchen with a confidence he wasn't feeling. But he was trusting God to put the words in his mouth. His approach slowed as he entered the dining area.

Miri was drying her hands on a towel. At any moment, she'd turn around, but he didn't wish to startle her.

"Miri." His tone was gentle.

She turned at the sound of his voice. "Michael." She sounded sad.

He'd been responsible for that. A new *fraa* should be thrilled at the sight of her beloved entering the room. "May we...talk?"

"*Talk*?" Her brow slightly rose along with the corner of her mouth. *She was teasing him?*

His heart soared. "Unless you have something else in mind." He smiled, his heartbeat quickening with each second, with each step she took toward him.

"They say the best part about fighting when you're married is you get to kiss and make up." She was *definitely* teasing. She curled her fingers around one of his suspenders and pulled him close enough to kiss. "I'm sorry."

He swallowed and nodded. "Me...me too."

Her palm planted on his chest. "Good."

Unable to help himself, one of his hands encircled her waist, pulling her against him, the other one instinctively slipped behind her head. He growled before their lips met, before they kindled more than just a flame.

"Wait." He tore himself away.

Her eyes opened, cheeks alive with color. "What is it?"

"I need to say something. Two somethings, actually."

"Say on."

"Make that three somethings. One. I love you like crazy, and I don't *ever* want to be without you." He kissed her on the mouth, then pulled back. "Two. I took a test and we're not HIV positive." He gently pecked her nose.

She gasped. "We're not?"

He shook his head. "And three, we have a court

hearing for custody of our son next month." He feathered tiny kisses across her cheek.

"We do?"

He nodded. "That was my other piece of mail."

"*Ach*, that's *wunderbaar*!"

He grasped the front of her apron and drew her near again. "I think *mei fraa* is *wunderbaar*." Instead of resuming their posture, he lifted her into his arms.

"Michael." She gasped as he continued toward their bedroom. "But it's the middle of the day!"

He closed the door behind them with his foot, bending to meet her lips. "Love has no timetable, *fraa*. And I'm sure *Dawdi* will understand."

THIRTY

The worst part about making a confession before the *g'may*, Miriam decided, was having to wait three hours till the end of the church meeting. How did they expect one to concentrate on the songs or sermons if they were anticipating their impending humiliation in front of their peers? Each second felt like a minute. Each minute, an hour.

She was glad that she and Michael wouldn't be allowed to attend the common meal afterwards. Surely, they'd be too ashamed to face everyone. Hopefully, by the end of the six-week *ban*, their friends would forget it ever happened. Not likely. Especially since they were attempting to get custody of their son.

The comforting part in all this was knowing that she and Michael were in the *ban* together. She couldn't imagine not conversing, eating, or sleeping with her husband for six weeks. She was quite certain that part was not in the Bible. *Nee*, it said what *Gott* had joined together let no man put asunder.

Michael attempted to send her reassuring smiles during the service, but she sensed his nervousness too. She couldn't wait for it to just be over.

The bishop finally stood up. "I'd like all the members to remain seated."

Miriam felt her cheeks growing hot. This had been the moment she'd been dreading, yet wanted to get over with, since first learning she and Michael would be making a confession.

All of the children and non-members filed out of Mose Borntrager's house.

"It was brought to the attention of the leaders that two of our members, Michael and Miriam Eicher, have been living in sin, to the result of producing a child out-of-wedlock. It is our duty to correct our brethren and sisters when they go astray." The bishop glanced at her, then at Michael. "If Michael and Miriam will now leave the building, the members will vote on a suitable punishment."

Both she and Michael rose and exited the building. She'd kept her head down the entire time. Now they would wait until they were called back inside. They were likely discussing the matter and taking a vote from each member.

One of the men called them back into the house. They each returned to their seats.

The bishop then gave the verdict. "The *g'may* has agreed that a confession and a six-week *ban* is sufficient. Please repeat after me...With heartfelt sorrow, I acknowledge that I have grieved *Der Herr* and the *g'may*. I now ask forgiveness and with the help of *Der Herr*, I will try to live a holy life."

Miriam knew the six-week *ban* was symbolic of Peter denying the Lord thrice, hence missing out on member privileges, such as sharing meals and voting, for three Sundays—every other week when their meetings were held. They were still required to attend the regular services, however. After the six-week *ban* had been fulfilled, their membership privileges would be reinstated.

They both repeated the bishop's words.

The bishop spoke again, "It is *gut* for you to once again be at peace with *Der Herr* and the *g'may*. We extend our heartfelt forgiveness."

No one spoke to them after meeting, except for a brief conversation with Sammy. They would walk home and allow Sammy to take the buggy. Miriam decided the fresh air and time alone with her husband would be beneficial for both of them.

"You're quiet." Michael spoke once they were out

of sight of the Borntrager's property. His fingers grazed hers, then they locked pinky fingers.

She met his gaze. "I never want to have to do that again."

He grunted. "*Jah*, me neither."

"Well, we got through it."

"I would think that wouldn't be any more difficult than going off into the *Englisch* world alone and having a *boppli* by yourself."

"*Jah*, you're right. I think that was the hardest thing I've ever done, next to giving our son over to strangers."

"Miri...I'm sorry."

"I know. Me too."

"Sometimes I wish I could go back and have a do-over. But I think I'd have to give myself a stern talking-to first. If only we had the wisdom we have now back then."

"I think the wisdom we have now is partly *because* of the mistakes we made back then, ain't so?"

He half-chuckled. "It's almost like God walks behind us with a broom and dust pan sweeping up the broken pieces of our lives. Then at a later time, He gives them back to us after He's fused them all back together. *Dawdi* told me to give God my brokenness and He would fix it. He was right. Little by little, all the broken pieces are coming back together."

"But it started with *Der Herr*, ain't so?"

"*Jah*. It wasn't until I surrendered to Him that He was able to repair what I'd broken. Like our relationship, Miri. What we have is something I only could have dreamed of." Tears shimmered in his eyes. "Yet, by the grace of God, here we are."

Miriam searched around for an extra table the next morning but couldn't find one. Perhaps Sammy only owned one. Which presented a problem. How were she and Michael supposed to eat separate from Sammy if she couldn't find an extra table?

"Michael, I can't find an extra table for us to sit at."

"We'll let *Dawdi* eat first. Then after he finishes, we can take our meal separately."

"Okay." She set a place setting at the end of the table for Sammy.

The creaking of the screen door told Miriam that Sammy had come in from morning chores. He moved to the sink and washed his hands, as usual, then walked to the table. Instead of sitting, he stared down at his plate.

"What's this?" He looked to Miriam.

"I can fill it for you if you just tell me what you'd like," she offered.

"*Nee*. Why only one plate?"

"Michael and I are in the *ban*, remember? We are not allowed to share a meal with you."

Sammy waved a hand in front of his face as though he were shooing away an insect. "I'm too old for this nonsense. I will not forfeit six weeks of the little time I have left with my *kinskinner* because some man tells me I can't eat with or talk to you. *Kumm*, you will eat with me. We can keep appearances in public, but I intend to do as *Der Herr* leads me in my own home."

Miriam cast a worried look in Michael's direction.

"The king has spoken. And you wondered where my mischievous streak came from." Michael laughed. "Bring the place settings. Besides, my stomach is growling."

"I don't want you to get in trouble, Sammy." Miriam worried her lip.

"I'm more concerned about the time I have left with you. Now, *kumm*, let us eat."

Miriam did as told, silently thanking *Der Herr* during the pre-meal prayer for this new wonderful family He had provided for her.

THIRTY-ONE

Michael and Miriam stared at each other in awe as the judge read his sentence. His official opinion stated that it was in young Michael's best interest to be returned to his biological parents. They had been granted full custody and guardianship of their son.

Prior to the court proceedings, the lawyer had informed Michael that his case would pretty much be open and shut. Since they were the biological parents, they had a stable home, and they did, in fact, want their child, she was almost certain they'd receive a favorable ruling.

Tomorrow, a social worker would arrive at *Dawdi's* farm with their son and all his belongings.

"Are you ready to meet our son?" Michael reached for Miriam's hand as they swayed on the porch swing. He was glad he'd taken the entire day off work, even though young Michael wouldn't be arriving till late morning.

"I am. I'm a little nervous, though. Do you think he'll like us?"

"I don't see why not. What's not to like?" He grinned. "Anyone would be happy to have a mommy as hot as you." His joke was completely lost on Miri.

"He's been *Englisch* his whole life. Do you think he'll like being Amish? Do you think he'll get along with the other *kinner* when he starts school next year? He's going to be different from them. He'll talk different. He didn't grow up speaking Amish."

"Hey, now. Why all the worry? *Der Herr* will take care of him, ain't so?"

"*Jah*, you're right."

He rubbed the top of her hand with his thumb. "Chances are, he's going to know us instinctually. He has our genes. You carried him inside for nine months. He might even remember your voice."

"Do you think so?" He noted the hopefulness in her tone.

"I do. There's a strong bond that doesn't disappear because of circumstances." He reassured.

"What time is Sammy coming back home?"

"He wants me to call the phone shanty nearest your

folks' place. They'll come meet their *gross sohn* at our word."

"Sammy will be his great grandfather."

"That's right. But he can call him Grandpa or *Dawdi*. It doesn't really matter." He squeezed her hand. "It looks like he's here." They waited for the vehicle to come to a stop. "*Kumm*, let's go meet him."

A woman stepped out of the car. "I assume you are Michael and Miriam."

"We are." Michael said.

"You certainly can't deny the resemblance. He looks so much like both of you." She moved to the back door. "Are you ready to say hello?"

"We are." Miri smiled.

The woman opened the car door and unfastened the straps on the car seat. "Michael, there two very special people here to meet you."

"Who is it?" Wide, curious eyes stared back at them.

The social worker set him on the ground. She gestured to Michael and Miriam to introduce themselves.

Michael nodded for Miri to go first.

She kneeled down in front of their son. "My name is Miriam. I'm your mom."

"You're my new mommy?" Excitement sparkled in his tone. He threw his small arms around her neck and kissed her on the cheek. "I love you."

Michael saw that Miri fought back tears and he massaged her shoulder. He crouched down next to them. "And my name is Michael. I'm your dad."

"Your name is Michael just like me? That's super-duper cool." He giggled.

Michael grinned and glanced at Miriam. "I think so too."

"How will they tell us apart if we got the same name?"

Michael exaggerated a shrug. "One of us could use a nickname."

"My old dad used to call me Mikey. But he went to be with the angels." He stared up into the sky. "Way up there past the airplanes."

"Do you like the name Mikey?" Miri asked.

The boy nodded several times.

"Okay, then, Mikey. I guess we've got that settled." Michael tousled the boy's hair.

"Mikey," the social worker said, "we need to get all your stuff out of the car. Do you think you can help me?"

"Yep! 'Cuz I've got big muscles like my new dad."

Michael chuckled. "I can help too."

The social worker looked at them. "I have a couple of papers for you two to sign. May we go inside? I'd like to take a look around, see his bedroom."

"Oh, uh, *jah*, sure." Miriam frowned. She'd never had a person from the government inside her home before. It seemed strange.

"Let's go show you your bedroom, bud." Michael hefted a large black garbage bag over his shoulder.

The social worker removed a bicycle from the trunk and set it on the ground. "He knows how to ride already."

Miri shared a worried glance with him. "It's okay," he mouthed soundlessly. Bicycles were not allowed in their Amish district. Acclimating their son to the Amish ways would take some time, but he aimed to make it as painless as possible for the boy.

Mikey hopped on his bike and rode it alongside Michael as he walked to the house.

"Just park that thing right here, bud." He gestured next to the porch steps.

Michael held the door open so everyone could file inside.

Miri led the way to the bedroom, followed by Mikey with his backpack, then the social worker and Michael, who each carried a large black garbage bag.

"Here it is," Miri said, holding the door open. "We can put your clothes in the drawers later, Mikey. And the toybox just has a few toys, so you can put the ones you brought with you in there too."

The social worker nodded. "And the bathroom?"

"Just down the hall," Michael answered.

"Very well. If we could just briefly review the papers I brought and get them signed, I'll be on my way." She smiled. "And the car seat stays with me. You'll need to purchase one, if you haven't already."

"Yes, we've already bought one." Miri and Michael shared a smile. Shopping for a car seat and toys had been a pleasure for both of them. It made their son's coming home all the more real.

The moment the social worker drove away, Michael walked to the phone shanty to call *Dawdi*. He'd been looking forward to meeting Mikey since he first learned about him. Miri's folks were anxious to meet their grandson as well. He'd left Miri to help settle little Mikey in while he made the phone call, but he couldn't wait to get back to the house.

As he entered the house, he heard Miri and Mikey talking in the bedroom. It sounded like they were putting his things away. Miri had made sure to bake cookies that morning so they'd have treats for their son and their guests.

He stood in the doorframe watching the two interact. *Ach*, he could hardly believe this was their son. And that he was actually living in their house now.

Mikey held up a die-cast toy and showed it to Miri. "This one's my favorite. It's an F16 fighter jet. I wanna fly one of these when I get big like my dad."

Miri glanced up and noticed Michael standing there observing them. Her smile was tentative. He could sense her mild anxiety. She was likely thinking what he was. How would they be able to get these *Englisch* ideas out of his head? Because last he checked, being a fighter pilot was nowhere near a suitable job for an Amish man. And although the *Ordnung* might change by the time their son became a man, it wouldn't change *that* much. He couldn't see the Amish ever embracing anything but non-resistance. And flying a jet of *any* kind? Not gonna happen.

"What do you say we taste one of your mom's cookies?" Michael clapped his hands and rubbed them together. Then he frowned dramatically. "Unless you don't like cookies?"

Mikey shot to his feet. "I love cookies! Are they choc'late?"

Michael led the way into the dining area.

"I made three kinds. Sugar cookies, peanut butter, and chocolate chip." Miri smiled.

"Uh oh." Mikey shook his head.

"Is something wrong?" Michael's gaze bounced from Miriam to their son.

"Yep." He nodded. "I'm 'lergic to peanuts."

"Oh, you are?" Michael frowned, looking at Miri. "Did they mention that? Is it in his paperwork?"

"I can check." Miri hurried to *Dawdi's* desk and found the large envelope left by the social worker. She pulled out the documents and scanned them. "*Jah*, it says so right here."

Michael crouched down in front of their son. "What happens to you when you eat peanuts?"

Mikey put both of his hands around his neck. "I can't breave."

A concerned look passed between Michael and Miri. "Well, we'll just have to be sure that the peanuts can't find you then." He reached over and tickled his son's belly. "No peanut butter spread for you, buddy."

"I made the peanut butter cookies last, so the others should be fine. I'll just put them away for now."

"Good idea."

Miri leaned close and whispered, "It also says he's afraid of the dark."

"It looks like a trip into town might be in order. I think they have those battery-operated push lights at the dollar store." Just then he heard the sound of horse hooves. "Oh, it looks like Mikey's got some visitors."

"I do?" He took the chocolate chip cookie Miri offered.

"Yep, your grandma and grandpa." Michael smiled.

"I never had a grandma and grandpa."

"Well, you do now. Let's go say hello." He reached for Mikey's hand. "Unless you wanna ride way up here on my shoulders?"

"Yeah! Just like an airplane."

Michael hoisted the boy up, and they all headed outside. "You're gonna have to watch your head when we walk through the door. Don't want to knock you out on your first day home."

Mikey giggled when he spotted the horse and buggy. "Why are they riding in a big box?"

Michael chuckled. "That's called a buggy. Maybe we can go for a ride later and you can see how fun it is."

"We can?"

"You bet. But right now, you can say hello to your grandparents." He lifted the boy from his shoulders and flew him down like an airplane.

"That was fun!" Mikey stared up at him in admiration, causing Michael's heart to swell with pride. It felt so natural having him here.

Sammy maneuvered the buggy to the hitching

post. He and both of Miri's folks exited the buggy, each carefully eyeing their new grandchild.

"How come Mommy and Grandma wear those funny hats?" Mikey leaned close and whispered in Michael's ear.

"Those are called prayer coverings or *kapps*. All the women around here wear them."

"How come?"

"To symbolize their submission to God. You will understand it better when you get older."

Mikey shrugged. "I don't get it."

"That's okay. You don't have to." Michael assured.

The grandparents came near and Michael introduced them all. "This is our son, Michael. But we have agreed to call him Mikey."

"Well, let's take a look at you, boy." Miri's *daed* sized him up. "Yep, it looks like you're going to be big and strong like your dad." He tweaked his cheek.

Mikey's mouth opened and he stared up at him in awe. "I am?"

"And just as good looking as your mom." Miri's *daed* winked in her direction.

"In that case, he's gonna have a tough time keeping all the girls away." Michael loved the tinge of color on his *fraa's* cheeks.

"I have a girlfriend at my preschool." Mikey beamed.

Miri laughed. "He sounds just like his *vatter*."

"You're going to have your hands full," Sammy said.

"For sure and certain," Miri's *mamm* agreed.

"I don't think Mikey's had the pleasure of meeting Dr. Seuss yet." Sammy smiled at Michael.

"Dr. Seuss? I love Dr. Seuss. He's my favorite book!"

"I think you mean author, bud. But this Dr. Seuss doesn't know how to write books."

Mikey brightened. "Does he have a wocket in his pocket?"

Michael chuckled and shook his head. He loved this kid's energy. He was so much like himself. They even shared a love of the same children's books. It was amazing how much they were alike.

"Does he like green eggs and ham?"

Michael scratched his beard. "I don't know. I've never offered him any. He likes carrots, though."

"*Kumm*, I'll introduce you." Sammy offered his hand and led Mikey to their horse.

As the afternoon passed, so did their anxieties. *Der Herr* had truly been at work and had smoothed out the path for their son to find them again.

EPILOGUE

Mikey's first month at home had gone better than they'd expected. He hadn't batted an eyelash when they'd switched out his *Englisch* clothes for the ones Miriam had sewn for him, although they'd kept his pajamas. As a matter of fact, he'd been excited to dress "just like Daddy and *Dawdi*."

Church, on the other hand, had been a bit more challenging. Four-and-a-half-year-old Mikey hadn't been used to sitting in one place for hours on end, and he hadn't liked being separated from his *mamm*. He'd wanted them all to sit together. Michael had kept him with him for the majority of the service, then ended up taking him outside during the final third. Toys and snacks hadn't proven enough to occupy him. But the leaders had been encouraging, noting that their children sometimes had problems sitting still. It was the way of children, they'd said.

On a non-church Sunday, the Pete Stoltzfus family had come to visit. Since their son was near in age to Mikey, the two boys had hit it off immediately. Hopefully, the boys wouldn't grow up to have a *rumspringa* like their wild fathers had. Miriam and Michael would definitely need to spend some time on their knees. They didn't need another heartbreaker.

The fluttering in Miriam's belly, more than just butterflies, reminded her that she had news to share with her husband after the others turned in for the night. After seeing Michael interact with Mikey, she was certain he'd make a *gut vatter* for their *boppli*. Right now, he was tucking Mikey in with their latest Dr. Seuss purchase. Perhaps they could sway their young son to become an author of children's books. The interest was definitely there.

She pondered these things as she removed her kerchief and let her hair down. She brushed out the tangles as a smile played on her lips. *Der Herr* had been so *gut* to her. In less than a year, He'd turned her entire life around. He'd given her things she hadn't known that she'd wanted or needed. But *He'd* known.

"I think he's out now." Michael whispered from the doorway.

She turned as he entered their bedroom and closed the door.

He sidled up behind her and took the brush from her hands. "May I?"

She nodded. He already knew she loved it when he offered to brush her hair. She relinquished the brush to his capable hands, closing her eyes, indulging in the gentle sweeping motions.

"Guess what? He wanted me to leave his light off tonight."

She half-turned. "Really?"

"*Jah*. He asked if Mommy and I used a light in our room. When I told him no, he said he wanted to sleep in the dark like Daddy." He chuckled. "Then I told him I'd leave the bathroom light on for him, but he assured me that he didn't need it anymore because now he had a headlamp like *Dawdi*."

She sighed in contentment. "He's growing up."

He moved her hair to the side and his warm lips dropped to her shoulder, meandering to her neck. "*Jah*." His voice lowered. "But I think he's going to get lonely. I think we should maybe...see about...a companion for him."

She grasped his hands and wrapped his arms around her midsection. "We've already got one on order."

He leaned back and stared at her. His mouth dropped open. "Are you...are you saying what I think you're saying?"

She nodded. "By this time next year, Mikey will be playing with his new brother or sister."

"*Gott* willing." He grinned. "And by the way things have been going so far, I'd say this is a pretty *gut* indication that He is." He shook his head. "All these things."

"What do you mean?"

"Well, when I first came back to the Amish, *Dawdi* encouraged me to read the Bible. He'd quoted that verse, *Seek ye first the kingdom of God and His righteousness, and all these things shall be added unto you.* I've never seen a clearer picture of that, Miri. And I'm not just talking about material things. He's done things I hadn't thought possible. He's placed love, joy, and peace in my heart."

"All these things." She grinned. "I like it. I think I'll claim that promise for myself. Although, I don't know what more *Der Herr* could add unto me."

Michael rubbed the place where their little one resided, happiness dancing on his lips. "Oh, I do."

THE END

Thanks for reading!
Word of mouth is one of the best forms of
advertisement. If you enjoyed this book, please
consider leaving a review, sharing on social media,
and telling your reading friends.

THANK YOU!

DISCUSSION QUESTIONS

1. Prior to growing into adulthood, veering from the path our parents brought us up on sometimes seems inevitable. Was there a time in your life when you rebelled? What did you learn from that experience?

2. Miriam carried bitterness in her heart because of past wrongs. Have you been through a season of bitterness? Have you relinquished it to God?

3. Regret can play a role in our ability to move forward. Is there something in your life you profoundly regret?

4. Have you ever known someone like Michael, prior to his recovery?

5. When Michael learns the reality of Miri's past, his focus immediately changed. Do you think

he was pursuing answers because of selfishness?

6. Would you have a difficult time trusting Michael, if you were in Miri's shoes?

7. Sammy seems to have advice for every situation, due to a lifetime of experience and studying God's Word. Do you have a "Sammy" in your life?

8. When Christ entered Michael's heart, He changed his desires. Have you accepted Christ into your heart? Has God changed your desires?

9. Michael eventually realized that seeking God's will was the key element missing in his life. Have you tried 'seeking first the kingdom of God'? What were your results?

10. God has adopted those who have called upon Him. Do you know anyone who's been adopted, physically speaking? Have you ever considered adoption?

11. Who was your favorite character in The Heartbreaker? Why?

A SPECIAL THANK YOU

I'd like to take this time to thank everyone that had any involvement in this book and its production, including my Mom and Dad, who have always been supportive of my writing, my longsuffering Family—especially my handsome, encouraging Hubby, my Amish and former-Amish friends who have helped immensely in my understanding of the Amish ways, my supportive Pastor and Church family, my Proofreaders, my Editor, my CIA Facebook author friends who have been a tremendous help, my wonderful Readers who buy, read, offer great input, and leave encouraging reviews and emails, my awesome Launch Team who, I'm confident, will 'Sprede the Word' about *The Heartbreaker*! And last, but certainly not least, I'd like to thank my ***Precious LORD and SAVIOUR JESUS CHRIST***, for without Him, none of this would have been possible!

If you haven't joined my Facebook reader group, you may do so here:
https://www.facebook.com/groups/379193966104149/

The next book in the series. *The Charmer (Amish Country Brides)*

The Charmer

Amish Country Brides

Release Date: July 1, 2020